T0207890

DANGER
ON THE
AMAZON

DANGER
ON THE
AMAZON

"A RICK SPEARS ADVENTURE"

ROBERT P. LONG

DANGER ON THE AMAZON
"A RICK SPEARS ADVENTURE"

iUniverse books may be ordered through booksellers or by contacting:

iUniverse
1663 Liberty Drive
Bloomington, IN 47403
www.iuniverse.com
1-800-Authors (1-800-288-4677)

Because of the dynamic nature of the Internet, any web addresses or links contained in this book may have changed since publication and may no longer be valid. The views expressed in this work are solely those of the author and do not necessarily reflect the views of the publisher, and the publisher hereby disclaims any responsibility for them.

Any people depicted in stock imagery provided by Thinkstock are models, and such images are being used for illustrative purposes only. Certain stock imagery © Thinkstock.

ISBN: 978-1-5320-0078-2 (sc)
ISBN: 978-1-5320-0077-5 (e)

Library of Congress Control Number: 2016912070

Print information available on the last page.

iUniverse rev. date: 09/21/2016

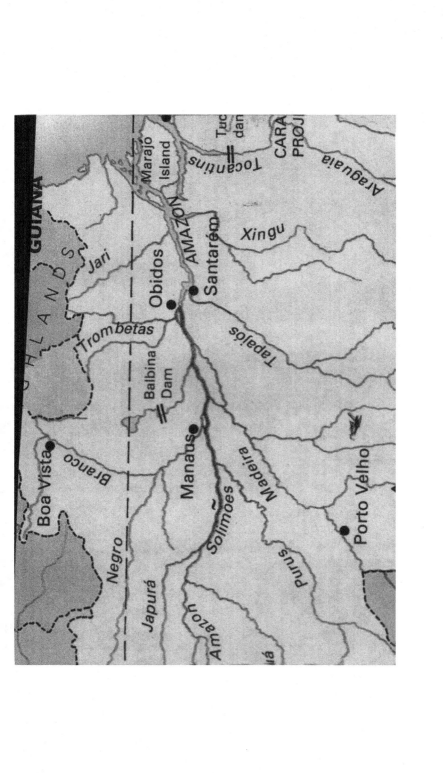

CONTENTS

Preface...ix

Chapter I   Hawaii 1

Chapter II   Alaska 13

Chapter III   North Dakota 24

Chapter IV   Mark and Joan in Hawaii............... 27

Chapter V   North Dakota 33

Chapter VI   Manaus, Brazil 41

Chapter VII   Launch Site............................... 47

Chapter VIII   Friendly Natives. 50

Chapter IX   Transient Natives 54

Chapter X   New Friends.............................. 57

Chapter XI   Black hulled boat 61

Chapter XII   Capture.................................... 66

Chapter XIII   New Friends.............................. 78

Chapter XIV   Parting.................................... 84

Chapter XV   Journey resumed 89

Chapter XVI   Motorboat thieves...................... 93

Chapter XVII   Helicopter................................ 104

Chapter XVIII   Final Landing............................ 112

Chapter XIX   Manaus, Brazil 115

Rick Spears was a writer for a sports magazine which featured his articles each month about fishing, and hunting small game. Rick had gone to a remote area in Alaska to live alone in the wilderness so that he could write a book about the experience from firsthand knowledge. He was accompanied by his good companion, "Bart", a large Malamute dog. Rick and Bart had fought off man and beast in Alaska.

The book had been completed and was doing well in sales.

He said that he had found three gems in his adventure in Alaska. The first was gold that he had discovered. The second was his friends, Joel and Jane, who had become his in-laws. The third was Mary, who had become his wife.

Rick had invited Joel to be his partner in mining gold. Their mining had been successful. They sold the mine, just prior to Rick and Mary's marriage.

Rick had made good friends in Alaska in addition to Mary, Joel and Jane. His new friends included: The brothers, Phil and George, fur trappers. Pete and Al who had helped him build his new cabin, and the Native Village tribe. Another of his good friends was Mark Hamilton, the buyer of his gold mine.

Rick had acquired one enemy. It was a man called Krazy Joe. Krazy had kidnapped and assaulted Dawn, a Native Village fifteen year old girl. Rick had saved the girl's life and had captured Krazy. Later, Krazy had burned Rick's first cabin.

Rick and Mary were married in front of his new cabin with nearly one 100 of his friends in attendance.

Now, they were leaving Alaska for their honeymoon, and a new adventure. It was October. After the wedding, Rick and Mary had arrived at Rick's home in North Dakota. Rick picked Mary up and carried her into the house. He kissed her and said, "Welcome home Mrs. Spears."

She returned his kiss and replied, "Thank you, Mr. Spears.

She took items from the car to the house, and Rick took the canoe, outboard, cart, and other items from the flatbed trailer to the garage.

Rick was in excellent physical condition. He had broad shoulders and a narrow waist. He was 6' 1" and weighed about 190 lbs. He was very strong.)

He admired Mary's beauty. She had a lovely smile, beautiful ash-brown hair, and carried herself with grace.

"Let us dress up and go to a nice restaurant. We're too tired to shop for food and then prepare it."

"What a beautiful idea. I'll be ready in three quarters of an hour.

He got out his Porsche. They went to a first rate restaurant. He asked for a quiet table. The waiter brought champagne. In the back ground pleasant music was playing. They ordered their dinner.

The food was exceptional. Afterwards, they danced. She asked that they play some of her favorites. They continued to dance, but It became late and they went home.

Rick asked Mary to use the internet to arrange for their flight to Hawaii in two days, and to arrange the return flight to Anchorage Alaska. He asked for first class if it was available.

She was accustomed to using the computer and the internet and accomplished the task easily. First class was available.

The day came. Rick called a cab and they were taken to the airport. The flight left on time and they sat side by side holding hands in first class. Mary was thrilled at the comfort and the service.

When they had been in the air at the proper altitude, the flight was very smooth. Rick said, "I'd like to discuss a possible adventure in Hawaii. Of course you are always welcome to come with me on my adventures. On most of them I will be writing an article for the magazine. I'll understand if a particular adventure is not to your liking, and you choose not to go along. This first one will be relatively easy. The weather will be mild, and it will only be for five days. Now, here is what it will entail. I'll go in this case to an uninhabited island with no food and no shelter. Some items I will take along that I will tell you about later. The object is to survive on what can be obtained from nature, and to learn how little one really needs is such a situation to retain good health. A boat would provide transportation to and from the island, and would pick me up at a certain date and time. What questions come to mind?"

"That sounds interesting. My questions are primarily about the items you would take along, and if I thought that I could do it successfully."

"Let's assume for the moment that you will be going along. I'll give to you my list of what I will take to give you an example. Then you tell me the several things that you wish to take. My several things are: A knife and machete combination, a zippo lighter, and a metal pot. What three things would you elect to take?"

"I:d want mosquito spray, suntan lotion, and water purifier tablets."

"Those are excellent choices. They're right in line with you background as a nurse. You will need to choose appropriate clothing. I'll take a wide brim floppy hat that can be put it water and then wrung out. Second, I will wear light weight khaki slacks, a long sleeve shirt, and one pair of canvas sneakers. Think about what clothing you would want to take. There are also a few things that both of us would need among them are T-paper, tooth brush and tooth paste, a bar of soap, and aspirin How do you feel about this adventure?"

"I'm excited about the idea, but I'm a little bit afraid. Fortunately, you will be with me. With your knowledge, I might be able to do it. If something unforeseen happened, of an emergency nature, what would we do?

"I'll take my cell phone to be used only for such an emergency. It's possible of course, that we may not get reception for the cell phone. In that case we will build signal fires."

"I'll go along. Now I need to think about the clothing that I'll take."

He reached over and kissed her and said, I'm delighted that you'll be with me on this adventure. You're a good sport, and I love you."

CHAPTER I

HAWAII

They arrived in Hawaii, and were taken to their hotel. It was beautiful. They had the honey-moon suite which overlooked the ocean. The management had provided them with a bowl of fruit, and chilled champagne.

The dinner was first rate. They danced.

It had been a long flight and they called it a day.

The next morning after breakfast, Rick asked at the desk what tours were available. There was a small bus leaving on an island tour in one half hour. On this tour the bus would stop briefly if asked. Rick signed them up for the tour. They went to their room to get cameras and a bottle of water.

The tour was delightful. Along the way Mary exclaimed, "Look at all the canoes. Let's stop to see them." They stopped and found that a canoe could be rented. Instructions were also available.

Rick explained to the operator that Mary was new to canoeing, and since they intended to canoe in various situations, Mary could probably benefit from their instruction. He explained that Mary would be in the bow. It was possible that they might encounter white water and rapids with rocks. Rick asked in their instruction could include those situations.

They said it did, and it would take a full day to complete the course.

Mary asked, "When would you be able to schedule me?

"Tomorrow morning at eight AM."

"I'll be here."

Rick reserved a small light weight, single person canoe for himself.

They continued the tour, marveling at the wonderful climate, the beautiful beaches and the very different scenery than that found in Alaska. They took many pictures. The tour ended just before lunch.

Rick suggested, "Let's rent a car and find a nice place to eat. We can eat some meals outside of the hotel, for some variety.

She agreed, and said that she wanted to go back to the room before they left.

On the way out, Rick asked for a list of events that they could review. The list included a concert, a stage show, and an art exhibit, and others.

They found a deli, and had lunch. That afternoon they had their own private tour which included taking more photos.

That evening they went to the art exhibit. This was a new experience for Mary. She was so pleased at the variety of experiences that she was having.

The next morning they drove to the canoe location after having breakfast in the hotel. Rick did not want to interfere in her instruction so he got his canoe, but kept an eye out for Mary.

After an hour he saw that the location would change for her instruction. A pick-up was brought up and they began to load her canoe on the overhead rack. Rick asked if they could also load his, which they did. They were taken to a more elevated area where there was a small river that was flowing rather swiftly. Rick noted that there were rocks in the water. It was an excellent river for a beginning course in white water canoeing. The canoes were unloaded and the instructor briefed Mary. When the instructor was ready, Mary got in the bow of the canoe and the instructor in the stern. They began to go down the river. Rick followed in his canoe. He could hear Mary squealing with delight, and was very pleased at her reaction. Along the way, he took pictures when he was able.

They stopped for lunch, and then the instruction continued until three thirty PM. when they returned to the canoe location.

Mary thanked them for the instruction.

"Rick, I just loved the instruction and the canoeing. I knew that I liked canoeing, and now I know more about what I can do to help while we canoe together."

"I'm happy about that. I'll have more to tell you later about a new adventure that I have in mind that involves canoeing."

Mary replied, "Great, I am ready to hear all about it when you are ready."

He had arranged for boat transportation to an uninhabited island for eight AM in the morning.

Early on Monday morning they had a large breakfast in the hotel dining room. They returned to their rooms and dressed for the occasion.

At eight AM they were boarding the boat. It took two hours before they arrived at the island.

The guide told them, "I remember seeing a nice little cove when I passed by here one time. Oh, there it is. He maneuvered the boat as close as he could to the beach.

They waded ashore and then waved goodbye.

Rick commented, "This is a nice little cove. We will come back here to be picked up. Let's look from here to see what the island looks like. First of all, there is a nice beach with beautiful white sand. The island appears to be mountainous, which is probably one of the reasons that it is uninhabited. The fact that it is mountainous is a good sign for us that there will probably be a stream where we can get fresh water. Then, just off the beach we see palm trees. Hopefully we will find coconuts."

"Let's walk down the beach to see what we can find. Every time there is a high tide, various things are left on shore after the tide receded. We may find things that we can use. Tell me if you see anything that could be useful."

She replied, "I see some driftwood. I believe that we could use it to build a fire, and I see netting, probably from a fish net that we might use."

"Great."

Mary said, "I see coconuts on some of the trees. They are up very high however."

He suggested, "As we walk along let us look toward the trees and see if we can pick out a good spot to make camp."

As they walked, she spotted an area in the trees where there was a small clearing. "Would that be a good place for our camp?"

"I believe that it would, let's walk over there and examine it up close. Yes, here we would have some shade, the ground is relatively level here and there is less sand here. You found a good one, if you will collect some fire wood, I'll see about making a shelter."

She got the drift wood. He found four trees that were six to eight feet apart. The area between them formed a rough square. Rick felled small trees, removed the branches and made a platform between the four trees about shoulder height.

He picked up the pot and they looked for a stream for fresh water.

They had been walking near the beach without success. He said, "Let's get to higher ground and then walk parallel to the beach. We may have better luck there."

They did not find fresh water. They returned to the camp. He asked her to walk along the beach to see if she saw any fish or other live things.

She returned saying that no sea life was spotted. She asked Rick about the platform.

"In the day time we can sit under it. We will add leaves on top and we will sleep up there at night. We do not know what animals are on the island, and it will be safer to be on the platform.

"How do I get up there?"

"It'll be my pleasure to lift you up."

He asked her to gather up leaves or other materials to make a relatively soft bed on the platform.

He took vines and made a cylinder of about two feet long. The one end had an opening of seven inches, more or less. The other end was closed. The cylinder was tapered from the seven inch opening to the other end which was about two inches in diameter. Spaces between vines were about one quarter of an inch. He then started a second one. She asked to finish it.

She asked what the cylinders were for. He replied that they were made to catch fish. It remained to be seen if they would work.

He took them out to where the surf was breaking and wedged them between rocks. Later he would check for results.

The next task was to get something to eat and to drink. She had seen some coconuts so they went to see if they could get them. They were beyond their reach. He cut down a slender tree, removed the limbs and attempted to knock them down. It was not successful.

He said, "I suppose that I will have to climb the tree."

"Rick, don't. If you fall, you could become seriously hurt."

"You're right; I will build a support belt that will also be of assistance in my climb.

He took a stout vine that was a little over ten feet in length. He went to the base of a tree, put the vine around the small of his back, and the tree, and spliced the ends together. This was an important tie, so he needed to strengthen it with tying smaller vines around the tie. She brought the small vines to him. He tied the middle of the large loop so that it formed the figure eight. On section was around the tree, and one around Rick. This was so that it would not fall while he was up in the tree. He began to slowly climb the tree, raising the vine on the tree with each step. His weight was divided between the vine at his back and his feet and knees. He reached the nuts, and knocked them down. Then the slow descent began, just reversing his upward maneuvers.

He used his knife and cut a nut open for Mary. She drank the milk. It was the first liquid drink since arriving at the island. He did the same, and then opened the nuts further and ate the meat. They both felt much better. He opened another nut.

It was fairly close to dusk. He wanted to check his fish traps to see if they had anything other than coconut for dinner. They swam out to the breakers. The fish traps were empty. They were left for checking in the morning. When they returned to the beach he explored the sand in the shallow water for clams or other sea creatures. He found a half a dozen clams. Using his knife he opened two of them. He went back to the fish traps and put one in each trap. He kept the shells, and returned to the beach.

They sat under their platform, cooked the clams and then ate them. The clams plus coconut milk and coconut meat was their dinner.

All in all, they had done pretty well. They had a shelter, firewood, food and drink. Tomorrow they hoped to find fresh water and to get some fish.

They walked the beach. They picked up the fish netting that Mary had found, and took it back with them.

He asked Mary how she liked self-sufficient island life so far.

"It has turned out better than I had imagined. Fortunately, you know what to do, and can do what is necessary. The island is so beautiful and I love this weather. It is such a change from Alaska."

They sat under the platform and talked. As it grew dark the mosquitos appeared and Mary used the spray.

Rick lit the kindling with his zippo lighter. As it caught and developed into a stable fire. He added some green leaves to produce smoke. The mosquitoes subsided.

Rick exclaimed, "There must be water around here somewhere. We will have to search again." Later, he placed some larger wood on the fire to keep it burning as long as possible. They were tired and Rick lifted Mary up to the platform. He climbed up also. Mary commented, "This is not too bad, but it is not like any mattress that I have ever used."

He agreed. "Perhaps we can get more leaves tomorrow and use the netting that you found to keep it in place. He suggested, "If you roll your hat up, you can use it for a pillow."

Mary replied, "I may do that later, but right now I want your arm around me. That will be my pillow."

Rick obliged, they kissed and slowly drifted off to sleep. They were awakened by low growling noises. As the noises came closer they sounded more like grunts. There was very little fire left, but they saw forms moving near the edge of the fire light. Now they heard grunts and an occasional squeal. Rick said, "Those are wild hogs.

Mary exclaimed, "I am glad that we are up here on the platform."

"That's right, wild hogs are dangerous. Now, if I had my rifle, or my pistol, we would have a roast for dinner. Of course, they are so big, and without refrigeration it would be a terrible waste. I will need to concentrate on something smaller."

The hogs had moved on. Now, how does one get back to sleep on a leaf covered wood platform?

They woke early in the morning, stiff and a bit sore. It had turned cool overnight. The fact that they were chilly woke them earlier than usual.

They got up and Rick lifted Mary to the ground.

Rick wanted to check out his fish traps and asked Mary if she wanted to go along. She said that she would gather fire wood while he went fishing.

He went out to the breakers and searched for his traps. He found them. It was a bonanza! There was a lobster in one, and a fish in the other. He picked up the traps with their contents and took them to the camp.

"Mary, look what I caught."

Mary was excited and said, "I'm so pleased that we will have a good breakfast. The firewood is ready to be lit."

"The clam bait is what made the difference. I will clean the fish and lobster. Will you cook them Mary?

Sure, I'll need to borrow your knife after you clean the fish so that I can get sticks to hold them over the fire."

The fish were cleaned the fire started, and then Mary cooked them. They each had half of a fish and half of a lobster. Things were looking up.

After eating, Rick took a slender tree that was about an inch and one half in diameter. It was about eight feet long. He sharpened the end with his knife. It was a spear to be used for defensive purposes.

They set out to see if they could find a water source. Mary carried the metal pot, and Rick carried the spear. This time they went to a higher elevation, and further from the beach. Eventually they found a small stream. The pot was filled and the purification tablets were added. They drank their fill of water and refilled the pot which they took back to camp. The water was boiled. Each day they made the trip to the stream and repeated the process. It was time consuming, but they were not complaining, they had water, fish and an occasional lobster in addition to the clams and the coconuts.

These events were repeated, and except for the hogs at night there were no problems.

They returned to the cove and waited for the boat. It arrived as scheduled and they were transported to the hotel. They immediately went to their suite. Mary said, "I am going to take a shower this minute."

Rick chimed in, "I will join you."

After a long shower, and then getting dressed, they went to the dining room for lunch.

During this week they went to shows and concerts. They enjoyed fine restaurants and drove to all parts of the island. One day they rented a canoe. They had the canoe delivered up stream to a launching point. They canoed downstream until mid-afternoon when they were picked up, and returned to the hotel. It was a busy week. The time came and they checked out of the hotel and got a cab to the airport.

On the plane they talked about the last three weeks. Although the shows and dinners were great, most of their time talking was spent about their week on the island, and their canoeing.

CHAPTER II

ALASKA

They arrived in Anchorage, Alaska. Joel and Jane were there to meet them. It was a happy reunion.

On the way to the Trading Post Rick suggested, "It is almost dinner time and we will be going right by Mark's restaurant. Let's have dinner there, and there will be no need to cook tonight or to wash dishes. I will treat."

Jane and Mary endorsed the suggestion. They entered the restaurant and saw Mark and Joan. This was another happy meeting.

Mark said, "We were just about ready for dinner, would you all join us?

All readily agreed and the waiter found them a good table.

Mark said, "Tell us about Hawaii and the things that interested you."

Mary explained, "I asked Rick to take me to Hawaii, and I am so glad that he agreed. It was wonderful. I took a course in canoeing, and we went to live on an island without taking food or shelter. It was so fantastic to live off the land for five days."

Rick added, "We also saw stage shows, went to concerts and art shows. We went to fine restaurants, and toured the whole island. We had the honeymoon suite at the hotel.

Joan remarked, "I love to canoe. I was on the canoe racing team in college.

Mark asked, "I want to hear more about the five day island adventured. I would like to go on an adventure like that."

Rick said, "We will tell you all about the five day island adventure. I don't know if you are ready for this, but I have in mind going on a new adventure soon. I haven't even told Mary yet, but it would be canoeing for up to one month on a river where there is no modern civilization as we know it. I do not have details yet, but if you think you are up to it we can discuss it further.

Mary said, "So that is the new adventure that you hinted at. I am all for it. The five day Island adventure sold me.

Mark said, "I am interested. Hearing about your five day island experience has got me going. We are young enough to experience something exceptional like this. What about you Joan?"

"I need more information, but I'm intrigued. Count me in unless something scares me out of it."

Mark ordered two bottles of wine. One red and one white.

The waiter took their orders.

Rick said, "The five days that we experienced was the first of this type of adventure. It was easy, only five days, and we had great weather.

Mark asked Rick, "What are your plans and your schedule?"

"We plan to visit at the Trading Post for a few days and then rent a car to go to our home base in North Dakota."

"Would you consider visiting with us at our home before going to North Dakota? We could talk further about adventures and find out more about what we would need. That would help us to decide if we could go along."

Mary said, "Let's do it, we are not in a great hurry, and I would like to visit them."

Rick agreed, "We will take you up on your invitation."

The food arrived. They ate and the talking slowed down.

When they finished, Mark said, "I'll take care of the check."

Rick responded, "Mark, I already invited them and said that it would be my treat."

Mary suggested, "Why not flip a coin for it? I have a coin. Call heads or tails. Rick called heads. Joel caught the coin. It was tails, Mark won.

They all thanked Mark and Joan, then said goodbye, and drove to the Trading Post.

Bart was so happy, wagging his tail and kissing Rick. Rick got on the floor and petted him. Mary joined them and they all enjoyed the reunion. Rick took Bart for a walk while Mary put their things in their room.

When they returned, Joel said, "Jane and I have been saving this champagne to celebrate your safe return. Joel filled the glasses and they all toasted.

Jane wanted to know more about the shows and concerts and restaurants. Mary obliged.

Joel wanted to know more about the island and their five day adventure. Rick filled him in telling him about the platform and the wild hogs.

Joel said to Rick, "I hesitate to ask you this question, but hearing of the adventures that you plan, I will ask. Jane and I have fallen in love with Bart, and have found that he is a wonderful guard dog. We will always have air conditioning, and would love to have him either on loan, or permanently. What do you think?"

"I can see your point. I believe that Bart would be good for you, and you would be good for Bart. Bart could not go along on the adventures that I have in mind. He is suited to the cold North, or to air conditioning. He could not survive in ninety degree heat. For now, I would say that all would be served well if I let you have him on loan."

"That would be great Rick. Jane will be happy about that."

Joel called Jane and said, "I asked Rick if he would let us have Bart on loan while they are going on their adventures and he said yes."

"Thanks Rick, "I'll feel better with Bart watching out for us."

"You're welcome Jane.

"Ok."

That afternoon, Rick finished writing his two stories for the magazine. One was about canoeing, and the other was about the five day adventure on the island.

That evening they talked about their plans. Rick and Mary would be leaving in the morning to visit Mark and Joan. Rick called Mark to confirm their visit and to get directions. He also called the brothers. This was a long conversation since they wanted to know all about Hawaii. He also called his business associates to bring them up to date.

Rick and Mary took Bart for their last evening walk. They were sad thinking of the parting, but knew that it would be best for Bart.

When they all returned they said good night and went to bed.

In the morning after breakfast they said a tearful goodbye. It was especially difficult to say goodbye to Bart. They promised to keep in touch by cell phone and drove off.

Arriving at Mark and Joan's house they saw what looked like a mansion. The grounds were extensive and well taken care of. There was a tree lined driveway which went to a garage in the back, as well as circling in front of the house.

They drove to the front and parked. Mark and Joan came down the steps to greet them.

Greetings were made, and Mark and Joan said that they were so glad to see them.

They went in and Mary commented about their lovely grounds and home.

Joan offered, "Let's take a little tour." They went through the living room, the library, the dining room and kitchen. In the kitchen a servant was preparing snacks for them.

Mark took over and said, "Let me show to you some things that I particularly like." He took them to the billiards room and then to the screened in swimming pool.

Both Rick and Mary complimented them on their beautiful home.

They went to the living room. A maid came in and took orders for drinks. When she returned she also had snack food.

Mark said, "I am so glad that you were able to take the time to come to see us."

Joan commented, "I can't wait to hear about your Hawaii adventure."

Rick replied, "Mary has told you about her canoeing course and our additional canoeing later. I will tell you about our five day island adventure. The purpose was to experience living off the land, without bringing food or shelter, and only a few items that we could carry. One becomes so used to buying all that we believe that we need, we do not realize that we have the capability to live a healthy life without them. We were taken by boat to the uninhabited island. We did not know what animals we would find. I built a shoulder height platform that we used as a bed at night. We sat under it in the shade in the daytime. The platform was built primarily for safety from animals. We found that there were wild hogs on the island. They are dangerous. We built fish traps and caught a lobster as well as fish. Mary spotted coconuts so we had the milk to drink and the meat to eat. We also found clams."

Mary added, "Rick took his knife, a zippo lighter and a pot to boil water in. I took mosquito spray, sun block lotion, and tablets to purify water."

Mark commented, "It is amazing that you took only a few things, and yet found food and survived."

Joan added, "It seems like a very difficult thing to do, yet, you accomplished it with ease.

Mary said, "It was not particularly easy but it was so rewarding. It gave me a new perspective, and a confidence that I did not have before."

Rick said, "I'd like to talk a little bit more about canoeing. "I know that you have had considerable experience in canoeing Joan. Mark could you tell me about your canoeing experience?"

"As a boy scout we used a canoe, but as an adult, I do not have experience."

"We have completed the first of our island adventures. I believe that it has been very helpful to Mary, as preparation for the month long canoeing adventure. She had a one day course in canoeing and then she and I rented a canoe for an additional day. I would like to suggest to you that a course would be especially helpful to you Mark in view of your limited experience. You see, when two of you are in a canoe, with one in the bow and one in the stern, you each have specific and different tasks than the other one. You two would need to decide after some training, which position each of you would be best suited for. For that reason Joan it would probably be good for you to go along with him. How does all that we have talked about sound to you?"

"I am not yet saying yes, but I am inclined to do exactly as you did. You showed us the way. We could go to Hawaii, take the canoe course and have the island adventure. What do you think Joan?"

"We both love Hawaii, and I love canoeing. I don't have knowledge about other uninhabited islands, and we know the weather would be great. We have the time, and what other week's activity would be so exciting? I say let's do it."

Mary added, "There are a few other things that we took along. T-paper, tooth brushes and tooth paste, aspirin, and soap. I don't know what we would have done without them."

The maid came in and whispered to Joan. Joan said, "Please come with me, lunch is ready."

As they ate, the conversation continued.

Mark asked for the name of the hotel, the name of the island, and the name of the boat owner who took them to the island.

Rick provided that information as well as telling them where the canoes were located.

Mark asked Joan, "How does our schedule look?"

"We are busy next week, but we have a clear schedule for the following two weeks."

Mark said, "I'll make reservations tomorrow morning. What kind of a schedule are you two on?"

"We will be going to my home in North Dakota. Then we will be making our plans. In addition to the adventures that I have told you about, our long range plan is to spend more time in a warm climate near water. I will continue to write articles as we go along for the magazine. It is not out of the question that I may write another book. The discussion flourished. After lunch, Mark invited them to play some billiards.

Mary said, "I will, if you can teach me. I have never played."

They gave her basic instruction. It turned out that she had a good eye for angles, and did well. They all enjoyed the game regardless of individual skill.

Mark said, "How about staying for dinner and then overnight? You can get an early start in the morning."

Rick and Mary looked at each other and nodded a yes.

Mary said, "We would love to."

Joan took Mary to a favorite room that she used to paint pictures of birds and wildlife.

Mark took Rick to his garage to see his cars. He had a garage for four automobiles. Joan had her own car. Mark had the Cadillac, a Rolls and a Mercedes. They then returned to the house and had a seat in Mark's den. He had a beautiful desk and comfortable leather furniture. On the walls he had hung his college diplomas and pictures of automobiles that he had owned. Rick saw that he had numerous pictures of the various gold mines that he owned.

Rick asked, "What are your plans for the mine that you bought from me?"

"It is too close to winter so I will wait until spring to bring in the machinery and the man power. My other mines are still working however. Soon they will all shut down for the winter. I am really looking forward to the Hawaii adventure. I have never done anything like that." Mark was a slender, six foot tall man. In his early gold mining days he had been physically active, but he had not been involved in physical activity for some time. He said to Rick, "I am not used to physical effort, I wonder if I will be up to the demands of the island and canoeing." Rick commented, "We will all need to prepare by taking exercises and canoeing. The easy five days in Hawaii will let you know what exercises that you will need.

I'd like to keep in touch with you and see how you and Joan liked doing something that is really out of the ordinary."

After they were served a superb dinner they retired to the living room. The conversation never faltered until late in the evening. The topic that kept coming back was that of the adventure in Hawaii.

It was late. They were shown to a beautiful room. They showered and went to bed.

In the morning they had breakfast and then said goodbye. They drove to North Dakota.

CHAPTER III

NORTH DAKOTA

After they had transferred their belongings to the house, and turned in the rental car, they returned home and sat down.

Mary suggested, "Let today be one of rest, conversation and eating out. We can go grocery shopping tomorrow."

"I believe you have the perfect schedule for today. We have had a busy schedule.

They went to a good restaurant for dinner. During the rest of the day and evening they talked and rested.

In the morning Rick finished writing his two articles. Then he said, "I believe it would be well for us to prepare our muscles for the river adventure. We may be canoeing as much as six or so hours per day. We'll need stamina and strength. Let's walk some distance each day. We can start with whatever distance that you are comfortable with, and then gradually increase it. We also need weight and shoulder exercise. It will probably take us a good two months to get in physical shape for the river. Do you have any questions or suggestions?"

"I like the idea of an exercise program. The thing that I would fear would be getting to a point where I couldn't physically keep up. My suggestion is that we get at least one pedometer so that we can keep track of our progress."

"Good idea. Let's make a list of the things that we will need to take along. Later, we can add to or delete items as we think of them. We should begin with the list we had for the island, and add to it. We'll need a map of the area that we will be in, a tent, sleeping bags, my outdoor cooking kit, a tarpaulin, and I will take my pump shotgun."

Mary added, "The one item that you mentioned that I do not have is a sleeping bag."

"Ok. I may have to buy one for myself too. The one I have is for cold weather and we will need light weight ones, as well as mosquito netting. We'll also need to take gifts for the village chief's. We'll need cash, ten's and twenties, plus inexpensive jewelry. I want to have extra zippo lighters to give to deserving people who are of assistance to us. We'll need non- perishable foods. I will also need to take binoculars, a small rod and reel, my snares, canteens, and a camera. Oh, and we'll need waterproof bags. If it rains, we'll need ponchos. Add whatever you think of to this list Mary."

"I'd like to add a very good first aid kit. In addition, an extra set of clothing each, plus extra underwear and socks. Also, I'll take pepper spray. I'll type this list on the computer, leaving space to add items. When we get close to the time to go I'll print it. If Mark and Joan go with us I'll print a copy for them."

"Thanks. Your adding the first aid kit reminds me. When we know the location of the river, we should ask about necessary shots for that area. We have a good start on the list. We can get the food items later. I also have binoculars and my exercise weights."

They went shopping and checked off items on the list until they had them. When they returned home they selected an unused closet to put all of the river gear in.

CHAPTER IV

MARK AND JOAN IN HAWAII

The next morning they walked before breakfast. The pedometer registered three quarters of a mile.

Rick and Mary began their three quarter of an hour exercise program. Mary used the two pound weights. Rick used his nine pound ones. They took their time and avoided over doing it. This exercise and the walking would be repeated five days a week.

During the rest of the week, Rick and Mary went to the library and began research to choose a river for their adventure. Their exercises continued.

In the meantime Mark and Joan approached the cove in their boat. The skipper took them in as far as he could and they waded ashore.

Joan remarked, "It looks just as Rick and Mary described it. It is so familiar I feel as though I have been here before."

Mark said, "Let's see if we can find Rick's platform. It will save me a lot of work if it is still standing."

They continued walking and saw driftwood on the beach and then spotted the platform in a small clearing.

Mark said, "I will gather some driftwood for a fire. I see where they made the fire. Would you gather some palm fronds and leaves to place on the platform please?"

After these chores were done they went to look for fresh water. They didn't find it after walking quite a distance so they returned of camp.

Mark said, "Let's look for coconuts. We will need something to eat and drink."

Joan exclaimed, "I saw some while we were walking, but they were up pretty high."

They found the trees. Mark cut a tall slender tree down with his machete and removed the limbs. He tried to knock the nuts down but the coconuts were up too high.

Joan offered, "Rick said that he climbed the tree to knock the nuts down."

"Yes, I recall that, but he also made some kind of a sling out of vines. I am not sure how that works. I will try to figure out another way."

He cut two other trees down, removed the limbs. He cut pieces of limbs of about two feet in length. Using vines he tied the pieces to the two trees to form steps of a ladder. He placed the ladder against the nut tree. Joan steadied the ladder while Mark climbed it and knocked the nuts down.

"Well done, said Joan. There is more than one way to get things done."

The nuts were split open. They drank the milk and ate the meat.

Mark asked, "Have you seen anything that looked like fish traps? Rick said that he had made some. I have no idea how to make them."

"I don't know what they would look like, but if we see something that looks like it was man made, that probably is it."

"He also said that they dug for clams and used the clams for bait, as well as eating them."

Joan asked, "Where would we dig?"

"I assume that it would be in the water close to shore. We'll just experiment until we find them."

He chose a straight branch and sharpened the end and began to dig near the shore. He bumped into something hard like a stone, and dug it up.

"Hey! He yelled. I dug up a clam. "He cut it open with his machete, and offered it to Joan.

Joan said, "It is awfully chewy."

"Sorry honey. That is the best we have so far."

He dug up more and opened them. He tried one and said you are right. I have got to find those fish traps. They both began the search, but did not find them.

Mark said, "Rick told us that he had anchored them in between rocks out by the breakers. Let's swim out there and look around."

They swam out and searched with their feet and looked with their heads in the water.

Joan came up sputtering, "I think I found them." She went under the water again and came up with two empty fish traps.

"That is first rate. Now I can put some clams in for bait and perhaps we will get something to eat. They swam back to shore, put the bait in the traps, and swam back out. They anchored the traps.

They had the platform, the fish traps, firewood, and coconuts. They still needed water so they went to search again. An hour later they found the small stream and filled their container. Joan put a purifying tablet in it. As they rested, they drank as much water as they could drink. They filled the container again and returned to camp.

That evening they lit the fire and sat under the platform talking about the day's events. Joan said, "Things are coming together and working out. I believe that we are doing fine. By the way, how am I supposed to get up on the platform?"

Mark replied, "I will lift you up just as Rick probably lifted Mary. Yes, things are going well. This is so new to both of us. We will learn a good deal from this adventure. Now, if we just have fish in the traps in the morning."

Later, they got on the platform to sleep. Joan commented, "This bed leaves a great deal to be desired."

Tiredness brought about a fitful sleep, but it was disturbed by snorts and grunts. Mark said, "Those are the wild hogs. I can't see details, but I see dark shapes moving."

The next morning they immediately swam to the breakers. One fish had been caught. It was cooked over the fire for breakfast.

The rest of the week continued without a major problem. They caught fish and dug clams. They ate coconuts and drank the milk.

They met the boat at the cove and returned to the hotel. After showering and drinking their fill of fresh water they went to breakfast for an enormous meal.

Next was the canoe headquarters. Mark explained that he didn't have canoe experience, and that he and Joan would be canoeing together. They planned to go on a long canoe trip which might include white water rapids.

The instructor asked Joan what her experience was. She replied. "In college I was on the girl's canoe racing team."

The instructor said, "That was a long slender canoe used only on flat water, is that correct?"

Joan replied, "Yes."

"Have you had any other canoe experience?"

"No."

The instructor said, "I would like for both of you to have separate instructors for the first day. This will be basic stuff. We'll try to decide which position each of you will do best in, and we will work on your strokes and explain the duties of each position. The next day you two will canoe in the same boat. We will also spend time on white water rapids. Do you have any questions?"

"Yes, how soon can we start?"

"Tomorrow morning at eight AM."

They agreed, and took the course.

CHAPTER V

NORTH DAKOTA

Back in North Dakota, Rick and Mary continued their research of rivers. They narrowed their search to Africa and South America. Their exercise program continued and the pedometer now registered one point two five miles per day. Each week they rented a canoe for an entire day. They took water and a lunch with them and spent the rest of the day canoeing. Their shoulders were becoming stronger. They were getting used to working together paddling the canoe. They occasionally added items to their list of things to take along. Coffee cups, and salt and pepper, for example.

One evening they received a call from Mark and Joan. Rick turned on the speaker phone so that they could both hear and speak.

Mark said, "We're back, and we had a great adventure."

Joan added, "I feel like a different person. It was such a great experience. Except for our honeymoon, it is the greatest time that I have ever had."

Mark said, "Thanks to your preparing the way for us with the platform and the fish traps, we had a great educational experience. Both of us have a different perspective about a number of things.

Joan added, "We both took the canoe course. It was two days long. I enjoyed every minute.

Rick said, "I'm so glad that it all worked out well for you. One never knows how a recommendation that is so different from one life style to another will work out."

Mary asked, "Did your island experience help you to make up your mind about going on a one month canoeing adventure with us."

Mark replied, "Indeed it did. We loved the five day adventure. We have discussed it and we are gung ho for the thirty day canoe adventure."

Joan said, "There is one thing that I would like to ask you guys to improve on the next adventure. If you build a platform, try to make it comfortable enough to sleep on."

Mary laughed and said, "I am with you on that issue Joan."

Rick said, "Now that we know that you are on board with the new adventure, we have some data to send to you. We have done some research in the library to select a few rivers to choose from. We have narrowed our original search to Africa and South America. Perhaps you could help us in that search."

Mary stated, "We have also come up with a list of things that each canoe should have. It is not a complete list, but it is a good start. I'll send it to you. Look it over and let us know what you think should be added or deleted."

Mark replied, "We will be glad to do that, but realizing how thorough you two are, I doubt if we will have much editing to do."

Joan told them about their search for the fish traps, and other things about the island.

Rick asked, "Did you decide which position each of you would have in the canoe?"

Mark replied, "Joan will be in the bow, and I will be in the stern."

Mary said, "That is exactly what we do."

Rick explained their exercise program to them and the reason for it.

They all talked some more and then agreed to talk again in one week after they received the materials from Mary.

Rick told Mary that he felt that they needed additional training in advanced white water canoeing. Mary was eager for the additional training. It was scheduled for the next week. The research of rivers continued.

Rick explained to the instructor that they had taken the introductory course in white water canoeing. They would be going on a long canoe trip where they might encounter vigorous rapids.

The instructor replied, "We have just what you want. In addition to swift water, and rocks, there will be whirlpools. I believe that with this course you will be well prepared.

They took the course and loved it.

Mary explained, "I was frightened, but learning what to do when we are close to crashing into a large rock, or about to be caught in a whirlpool, gives one confidence."

A week later Mark called. He told them that he was on the speaker phone so that Joan could hear.

Joan said, "Hi, we received your list of items to be taken along. It was very complete. I have added pepper spray as you did Mary, and I also added sun glasses.

Mark added, "I will take a twelve gage, pump shotgun as well as sunglasses. We have also started to walk more and to exercise. This is turning out to be quite an undertaking.

Mary offered, "I believe that we should also take anti-biotics. We can get them in pill form. Your doctor can prescribe what he thinks that you need when you ask him about shots."

Rick said, "I am glad that we are all getting involved in preparations. It's an exciting thing that we are going to do. My research has led me to lean toward going to Brazil in South America. The Amazon River is there. You might want to go on the internet or to the library to learn about it. Then you could compare it with other rivers that you believe that we should consider."

Mark asked, "Do you have an idea as to how soon we will need to be ready to go?"

Rick replied, "I do not have a firm date at this point. I suggest that we tentatively think of arriving in South America about the first of January. The dry season begins in December. Incidentally, I have mentioned canoeing for one month. We will not know until we are there how long we will stay. The circumstances at that time will probably decide for us how much we will want to see and do. Have you come up with rivers for us to consider?"

Joan replied, "We have used the internet. We thought about rivers in the US, but took them off the list as not being remote as you had suggested. We thought about the Niger river in Africa and the Amazon in South America."

Mark added, "Either the Niger or the Amazon would be satisfactory to us."

Rick suggested, "Let's gather more data on the Amazon then, and firm up our decision in about one week."

All agreed. They said goodbye.

Rick's research revealed that Manaus was probably the best city for them to arrive in Brazil. It was near the Amazon, and near the center of Brazil. At that point they could get a guide who would take them and their canoes to a launching point on one of the tributaries leading to the Amazon. The tributaries were coming off the mountains. Fishing was reputed to be good. The waters may be white water with rapids however.

Rick looked into canoes. The natives used large heavy canoes made from hollowed out trees. They could carry an enormous load, but were not very manageable. Canoes in the US were made from various materials, wood, aluminum, fiberglass, a material called Rolex that could be bent but would bounce back into the original shape. It was very heavy however, and since they might need to carry the canoes around dangerous rapids, the weight ruled them out, as it did the wooden boats.

Rick told Mary about his findings, and that he preferred the modern US boats that had lightweight materials such as fiberglass and Kevlar.

Mary agreed, but asked, "How do we get them to South America?"

"I believe we can order them from the manufacturer and have them delivered in Manaus, care of the guide. I'll ask Mark if he could handle that detail."

Rick called Mark and Joan, telling them about the town of Manaus, and his research on canoes. He went into detail about the canoes with Mark, and asking him to arrange the purchase, including paddles and life jackets, and delivery to their guide, Carlos.

Mark said that he would make the arrangements and wrote down details of the guide's name and phone number. He also got the name and specifications of the canoe and the name and phone of the manufacturer.

Joan remarked, "We have bought everything that we know that we will need and are looking forward to our new adventure."

Mary agreed, "I too have been eagerly awaiting the start. Now we will need to make plane reservations. We will also need hotel reservations in Manaus. I'll take care of those for us."

Joan added, "I'll make our reservations."

Rick suggested, "We might want to get to Manaus a couple days early in order to meet the guide and to make final arrangements. We may also get local advice before we leave with the guide."

Mark summarized, "That means that we have about two and one half weeks before we leave."

Rick said, "I'll call again in about a week to make certain that we are on the same page."

They all agreed and then said goodbye.

A week later Rick called Mark and Joan, using the speaker phone. When they were all ready to talk, Mary told them, "I have made airline and hotel arrangements for Rick and myself. We are to arrive at the hotel at the beginning of the last week in January."

Joan said, "We are scheduled to arrive at noon on Tuesday of that week."

Rick said, "I have talked with the guide and told him of our arrival. He knows of a good launching location that he can take us, our canoes and other gear to. He says that it has been raining but it was beginning to slow down. Mary and I are taking ponchos rather than rain jackets."

Mark responded, "We will be checking our list. It seems to me that we had jackets. I suppose that sitting in a canoe, while it is raining, one would be dryer with a poncho. Except for that item I believe that we are ready. By the way, I got one canoe in red, and the other in tan. You may have your choice."

Mary replied, "I would like to have the tan one."

They talked a bit more, and said that they would meet at the hotel in Manaus.

Rick and Mary saw the doctor and got the necessary shots and antibiotic tablets.

CHAPTER VI

MANAUS, BRAZIL

Rick and Mary *flew to* Manaus. It was raining when they arrived. They checked into the Raquel Wellington hotel. They had lunch in the hotel dining room. Rick asked at the desk if tours of the city were available. The answer was no, but it was suggested that they hire a cab to drive them around. Emanuel was suggested as their driver. The desk located Emanuel. He arrived and welcomed them. They drove around seeing where the nearest grocery store and other places of interest were. Emanuel told them that the weather report called for sunny weather tomorrow.

Rick called Carlos and asked him to give them a briefing at 9 AM on Wednesday morning.

Mark and Joan arrived on Tuesday as scheduled and checked into the hotel. After they had eaten they met with Rick and Mary in the lounge. Rick told them of the meeting with Carlos at 9AM the next morning. They were all excited about being so near to starting their canoe journey. They had dinner together in the hotel dining room, and talked until it was obvious that the waiters wanted to clean up and leave. Other diners had already left. Talking was continued in Mark's room until they were all ready to turn in for the night. After breakfast they met their contact in Rick's room.

Carlos shook hands with everyone. He said, "Rick asked me to tell you about the area, the natives, the wildlife and the river. You are about to have an adventure of a lifetime. I hope that you have prepared yourselves physically and mentally. It will be physically demanding and there will be danger. I'll brief you on what to expect. If you are aware of the possibility of a problem, you may be able to avoid it. This is a wonderful opportunity to see the scenery, the natives, and fish and land animals that will be different from what you have ever seen before.

Good landings are few and far between. I have a copy of a map of the area for each of you. It shows some landings where I know the natives."

"There is no local law here, no 911 to call. I know you are armed. Let people see your guns. The word will get around, and you will be safer for it. The size of you men will also discourage those who are looking for trouble. Four years ago in 2009, a 21 year old man was killed in western Brazil. A witness to the attack said that the victim was partially eaten by the natives.

Rick said, "How likely is it that that sort of thing might happen where we will be going?

"In your case, it is unlikely. Preparation and alertness on your part will be your protection. You are armed, physically fit, you are aware, and you are not traveling alone.

Tribes fight with each other, and some are hostile to strangers."

Joan said, "You scared me. I didn't know that the natives were so wild."

Mary said, "I was afraid of the white water canoeing lessons, but it all came out ok. I believe that this will too."

Carlos said, "Yes, I believe that with your preparations and serious attention to possible problems that you will do well. You will be in a rain forest, with tributaries and the river running through it. Generally, the vegetation comes right up to the water edge. Landings are at locations where the vegetation is sparse. You may canoe for hours before you find a suitable place to land. I have seen your canoes. They are beautiful and the natives would love to have them. I suggest that you do not leave them in the water overnight. Put them near your tents. Have some kind of an alarm system on them, or they will be gone in the morning."

"You will be starting on the north end of a tributary coming from the mountains. The rainy season ended at the end of last month, and the tributaries are almost back to normal. As you canoe, you will encounter fast water, rocks and whirlpools."

"You will be able to catch fish. There are many dozens of kinds of fish. Some of them are dangerous, like the piranha. They attack as a group. In twenty minutes or so, they can completely devour an animal the size of a good size dog. Electric eels are powerful, with 100 volts per foot of length. Some grow to 7 or 8 feet. That would produce a lethal shock. There are different kinds, but most are shaped like a long sausage. They breathe air, and must come to the surface for a breath frequently. Do not let your hand or foot hang out of the canoe into the water."

"The first landing will be on your left side about six hours after you leave from the point where I will take you. There will be a native tribe there that is somewhat civilized. I have met with them and told them of your arrival. From that point on you will have to pick your landings and be prepared for tribes that may be hostile."

"There are many land animals that you can hunt to get meat. There are ant eaters, capybara, tapirs, monkeys, and birds of all sizes. When you are hunting, watch where you step. There are many poisonous snakes. In addition there are anacondas and jaguars."

"If the natives like you, they will probably give you something to eat. I suggest that even if you do not like the looks of it you eat it, or they will be angry. I am certain that you have already obtained small items to give to them. You should have basic eating supplies with you in the event that the natives don't feed you or that you do not catch fish or shoot game."

"You may see natives in boats that have large outboard motors. Steer clear of them. The average native cannot afford a motor or gasoline. Those with motors are frequently thieves, counting on the speed of their boats to escape capture."

"The rivers overflow, and the water can go for miles on either side, and the water may rise as much as 30 feet. At that time, fish swim among the tree branches. Of course, that is over for this season. When the water recedes, pools will be left, in some places, on either side of the tributary and fish may be stranded there. They will be easy picking for your dinner. I am sure that you all know to boil the water."

"There is one other thing that I wanted to tell you. Your former president, Teddy Roosevelt, took a canoe trip on the Amazon just as you are doing. Of course, he had a large group of people with him. He had malaria and an infection and nearly died."

Mary asked, "If an emergency arises, whom can we contact?"

"The best bet would be to contact the nearest tribe. If it is an injury, their medicine man may be helpful. I have contact with some of the semi-civilized tribes. Through them I can keep track of your progress. They can also get a message to me if necessary. You understand, all of that will take time."

Mark asked, "When will you be ready to take us?"

"If you wish, I can have the canoes and your other items packed and ready to leave your hotel at 9 AM tomorrow. It will take us three or more hours to get there. Would that be ok?"

They all agreed and thanked Carlos for the briefing, and said goodbye.

Rick said, "Except for the snakes, I believe that we have chosen the right river and the right guide."

Mark added, "We wanted an exciting adventure and it looks like we're going to get it."

Mary said, "Yes, and I'm glad that we took the time to properly prepare.

Joan said, "You all are so positive, but I am a little scared."

Rick said, "You'll be fine after we get started. Does anyone want to go to the store for a last minute item or two? They did, and each found what they needed, including bells to put on the canoes.

Afterwards, they went to dinner. Conversation lasted all evening.

They retired, thinking that this may be the last good sleep they would have for a month.

CHAPTER VII

LAUNCH SITE

Carlos delivered them and their gear to the starting landing. It was about two thirty pm. They decided to start canoeing the next morning.

The tents were put up. Upon looking around, they could see that the scenery was beautiful with many shades of green. Bright colored macaws flew overhead. All of the beautiful colors made the women think of dresses they would like to have with those colors. They could hear monkeys chattering. Mary and Joan took pictures. The river was fairly narrow, and ran swiftly, but it was not a problem. This is what they had come for.

It was warm, probably about 85 degrees, and humid. It got them sweating. They were not used to this rain forest climate. In the morning it would be cooler. They unpacked their gear and sorted it all out, then packed it in their canoes. They gathered wood. They started their fire, intending to keep it burning until they left in the morning.

Later, Rick went fishing. He got four fish. They were so different from those that he was used to. Several of them had huge teeth. He was fascinated by their appearance and took pictures of them. He gutted the fish, but left the heads, tails, and scales on them. The fire was pushed aside. The fish were wrapped in leaves, placed where the fire had been, and then covered with the embers to cook. Water had been boiled, and rice was added to it. Each person had a whole fish and rice. Dinner was proclaimed to be a success.

After dinner they sat around the fire and talked.

When the mosquitos appeared, they sprayed each other with mosquito spray. Additional wood was placed on the fire, and green leaves were added to discourage the mosquitos.

They talked until they were tired, and then rolled out their new sleeping bags in the tents, and went to bed.

After breakfast Rick strapped the shotgun on his canoe where he could reach it easily. He had ammunition for birds or for larger game. The fishing rod was easily accessible also.

The canoes were placed in the water and they shoved off. The water was swift and there were rocks, and overhanging branches to avoid. Rick and Mary were in the lead, and Mary pointed out the birds and other animals that she saw. She was having fun singing the "Yellow Bird" song and laughing. Rick was pleased with her positive and cheerful attitude.

About noon Mary saw a small clearing and said, "There's a great picnic spot, it is level and doesn't have much brush. Let's stop for lunch."

Rick agreed, and motioned to Mark and Joan to follow. They tied the canoes up, and got out and stretched. They had been canoeing for a bit over three hours. For lunch they had power bars and some hardtack candy. Water they got from their canteens.

After a 30 minute lunch break they began canoeing.

About an hour before dusk they felt that they were probably near the landing where the friendly natives were. They saw smoke, and then the landing

CHAPTER **VIII**

FRIENDLY NATIVES.

They beached their canoes and got out. Children came first, laughing and pointing at their canoes. Then the adults came to see them.

Rick asked for the chief, and a man came forward wearing only shorts. He had flowers around his neck, and what looked like animal teeth around his nose and ears. Rick gave him a twenty dollar bill, and a lighter. He demonstrated its use. The chief showed them where they should put their tents. He then took them to see the large community hut. It was open sided and had a thatched roof. Each family had an area near the outside edge of the hut. They had their own fire, and hammocks were used for sleeping. There was no provision for privacy. As they walked around they handed out costume jewelry to the natives.

Children did not wear clothing. Most men had a thong or wore shorts, but some did without. Most of the women wore skirts or shorts.

They brought their canoes up to the location that the Chief had indicated. They erected their tents. Mark made the fire.

Many of the natives had followed them and watched the activity. Then Mary noticed that they were staring steadily at something. She said, "Joan, they are staring at your beautiful platinum blond hair. They have probably never seen hair like that before." Then Rick and Mark also noticed the staring.

Rick said, "You are a celebrity Joan."

The natives continued to stare, and many sat down on the ground for an extended stay. Joan was tall and slender. In her younger years she had been sucessful in beauty shows.

Mary said, "Think I'll check our boat and install the bells."

Rick said, "I'm going to take a look around the landing." He returned shortly, and motioned for Mark to join him. "Mark, I just noticed that there is a black hulled boat with a large Mercury outboard on it. It looks like the ones that Carlos told us about. It is about 22 feet long. It is slender and it looks fast."

Mark said, "We had better keep our eyes open.

Rick agreed and they returned to the tents without mentioning the boat.

Four women came from the main hut. Each held a large leaf, somewhat larger than a dinner plate, with food on it for each of them. They thanked the natives.

Mark said, "Does anyone know what this food is?"

Joan replied, "It looks like vegetables, and I see sweet potatoes. In any event, let's eat it."

Mary said, "I think you are right. It tastes pretty good."

The onlookers continued to stare until called to dinner.

Rick said, "It is nice to have time to eat without being watched each minute."

Within ten minutes the natives were back, sitting on the ground, watching. This continued until Mary said, "Let's go to bed, we have another long day ahead of us." The natives then went to their hut.

They got up early, and after breakfast, thanked the Chief and shoved off.

Rain clouds appeared, and they got their ponchos out. The dry season had arrived, but they could still get showers at any time. The rain began, but they were prepared. By noon the rain had stopped and they found a place to tie the boats. They got out and stretched.

Mary said, "Let's have tuna and Triscuits for lunch."

Rick mentioned to Mark that the black hulled boat had left before they did.

They continued their voyage. At times the river narrowed and the water flowed swiftly. There were rocks and whirlpools. Mary was excited and laughed and cheered when they avoid a large rock or a whirlpool. Rick had a broad smile, enjoying Mary's enthusiasm.

Joan was intently concentrating on studying the river and paddling. She heaved a sigh of relief when they were in calmer waters.

CHAPTER IX

TRANSIENT NATIVES

They had been looking for a landing without success. It was about an hour before dark, and they would have to find a place soon. One half hour later Mary saw a small landing ahead. There was no other landing that they knew about within a day's travel. Rick motioned for Mark and Joan to follow and brought the canoe up to the land. Naked children came out, but there were no smiles. Adult natives also came to look. There were no greetings. The adults did not wear clothes, and had markings on their faces similar to what the American Indians had.

Joan said, "Why don't we just canoe further on?"

Rick said, "It is almost dark. It would be dangerous to continue, not being able to see where we were going. Let's put on a brave face and go on. Let's get our guns out right at the beginning Mark."

Rick held his gun in his left hand while he pulled on the bow with his right. Mary pushed from the stern and they got the boat up on the land. Mark followed and they chose a camp site.

Rick said, "Let me talk to your Chief please."

A rough looking Chief came up. He did not wear clothing. He had a necklace of different kinds of teeth, and markings on his face.

Rick offered to shake hands but was ignored. He offered a lighter to the Chief, and demonstrated it. The Chief took it then turned his back and walked away.

These natives must be transients, for they did not have a hut, just temporary lean-tos. Costume jewelry was handed out.

Tents were raised, and a fire was made. They had brought the boats up very close to the tents and installed their alarm system.

Dinner was made from their reserves. These natives also watched them eat and stared at Joan's hair. Rick noticed that a few of the men talked together while staring at Joan.

They went to bed early to avoid the stares of the natives.

In the morning the tents were taken down and the canoes were packed.

They put the canoes in the water, resuming their journey. At noon they took time to talk about last night's camping. They were all pleased to be away from the sullen natives. Joan said, "I was afraid of them. I hope we find a camping location by ourselves, or one with friendly natives."

That afternoon they found a small clearing and no one was around. They set up their tents, and pulled the canoes up beside them.

Rick said, "I'm going to see if I can get something for dinner other than fish or our reserves." He took his shotgun and went into the forest. Later they heard his shotgun fire. Mary said, "I wonder what he got." Rick returned with a bird about the size of a small turkey. Mary boiled water." They used the boiling water to soak the feathers, making them easier to pluck. Mark made a rack to hang the bird from to roast it.

It took quite a while to roast the bird, but it was worth it. They all had a second helping.

CHAPTER X

NEW FRIENDS

In the morning they shoved off again under a clear sky. Around noon time they overtook a native man and a woman in a dugout canoe. As they came along side they said hello and the natives smiled and greeted them. Both wore shorts.

Mary asked, "Do you live in this area?"

The man replied, "Yes, our tribe is just ahead about one hour from here. Where are you going?"

Rick said, "We are on vacation from the United States, and we plan to spend another three weeks canoeing towards Manaus before we return home." He introduced everyone and asked for their names.

"My name is Manuel, and my wife's name is Ana Maria. Our tribe is friendly, and we would like to hear about the area where you live. Come to our camp, and you can learn about us, and we can learn about you."

Rick said, "Yes, that sounds like a good idea. We'll follow you."

When they arrived at the landing, children and adults came to greet them. There were smiles and greeting of hellos.

Manuel introduced them to the chief, who welcomed them and said, "Manuel has been a teacher in Manaus. He is from our tribe, and has returned here to educate us. We are honored to have him with us and to have you visit us. Let me show you where you can put your tents. When you get set up I will take you on a tour."

Rick gave him a twenty dollar bill and a lighter. The chief thanked him and left them to set up their tents.

After setting up the tents and bringing the canoes alongside, Manuel took them to the chief. He showed them the main hut. It was similar to what they had seen before, but there were bamboo partitions between each family's space. It provided some privacy. Most of the natives wore shorts, while some women wore skirts. Very few had paintings on their faces. Many had necklaces.

Mary and Joan handed out items of jewelry. Some natives thanked them. In the center of the large hut there was a fire.

After the tour the chief asked them to have a seat near the fire. He joined them and invited Manuel and Ana Maria to be seated also. He said, "We will eat soon and you are invited to join us for dinner. We want to hear about the area where you live, and something about how you spend your time."

Rick told about his writing, and Mark told about his gold mines. Mary said that she was retired but had been a nurse. Joan told about her schooling and how she liked canoeing. Mark told them about the snow and the cold temperatures in Alaska.

The chief asked about their ages. Rick said that he was almost 49, and the others gave their ages. The Chief was surprised as were the natives that they were so old. The chief said he thought that he was old at the age of 39. He said that he had been to the big city of Manaus, but that he had not been out of Brazil.

Food was brought to them. It was similar to what had been served to them before, but with it was a fillet of fish for each. They all found it to be delicious.

The evening passed with them all answering questions. Then they said thanks and retired to their tents. The bells were set and they went to bed, happy to have been in friendly company, and having a fine dinner.

In the morning Manuel came to their tents and asked if they would stay for another day. He said, "It would help the children so much if each of you would give a short talk about things that the tribe knows little about. It would help to round out the information that I have been giving them."

Rick said, "We don't have a specific deadline. What do you all think?"

There was agreement to accommodate Manuel.

Manuel said, "The children's class will start in about one hour in a hut behind the main hut. Would that time be alright for you?"

"Yes, we'll have breakfast and then we will come over."

They joined Manuel and the children and gave their talks. Rick told them the story about the grizzly attacking him. Mary told them about work as a nurse in a busy hospital, Joan told them about the education system in America. Mark showed them how to pan for gold by a small stream. He found a few specks of gold to show to them. When they returned, their questions continued and a number of adults joined in.

Finally Manuel said, "Thank you so much for taking your time to speak to the children. It is almost lunch time."

He excused the children and then invited his guests to have lunch with him and Ana Maria.

Manuel said, "Here is my phone number. Perhaps we could get together in Manaus before you go home. I plan to be back there in about two weeks."

They agreed to call him.

In the morning they said goodbye to all, having enjoyed their visit. It was an unexpected pleasure to enjoy the company of friendly natives. They packed up and resumed their journey.

BLACK HULLED BOAT

During the next week they enjoyed good weather, friendly natives and landings where they were alone. The fishing and hunting was good. One day they observed an electric eel shocking a fish in shallow water and then swallowing it whole.

The next landing seemed to be a repeat of the one with the transient natives who were almost hostile. It was near dark when they approached the landing. Once again they saw the black hulled boat with the large Mercury outboard. These natives were more than sullen, they appeared to be angry. The naked children threw rocks at them, and the adults did nothing to stop them. Once again they would have preferred to travel on, but it was near dark and too dangerous to canoe.

They got out of their canoes, and holding their shotguns in one hand, pulled the canoes up with the ladies help.

Rick asked to speak with the chief.

When the chief arrived, Rick gave him a lighter and a 20 dollar bill. The chief accepted them and said, "What you want?"

Rick said, "Where should we put our tents. We will stay tonight and leave in the morning."

The chief made a vague gesture in one direction and left.

Rick said, "OK, we are on our own. Let's pull the canoes over to where we will raise the tents, and get squared away."

As they erected the tents, natives, came, as before, to watch their every move. Once again they stared at Joan's platinum blonde hair.

Joan said, "They give me a creepy feeling with their staring."

They set the alarm system on the canoes and had a hurried dinner from their reserves.

They went to bed to avoid the natives.

In the morning, after a cold breakfast and packing to leave, Rick left the camp to check the landing site. The black hulled boat was still there.

When he returned to the camp he asked where Joan was.

Mark said, "She's on a bathroom break."

They took the canoes to the water's edge, but Joan had not returned.

Mark took his shotgun and said, "I'm going to go find her."

Mary took her pepper spray and went with him.

They returned without her.

Rick said, "The black hulled boat is gone, I believe that Joan has been kidnapped. Let's go to the next landing which has friendly natives and have them contact Carlos."

Mark said, "I can't do that. What if she is just lost? Let me ask the chief for his help."

He returned shortly and said, "The chief will not help."

Rick said, "I don't believe that she could be lost. The river is right here for a landmark, and she could hear the sounds of the camp. I really believe that she has been abducted. Let's go to the next landing."

Mark didn't want to go, but he had no choice.

They got in their canoes and left.

After a few hours they stopped at a clearing, to stretch their legs and to get a bite to eat.

Mark said, "I know that I am holding you back because I can't paddle as fast as you do. Why don't you go on and get things started at the next landing, and I will get there as fast as I can."

Rick said, "OK, I'll call Carlos and let him know that we are coming." There was no answer.

They raced to the next landing.

When they arrived, they went ashore and told the story. They asked the chief to contact Carlos. He sent a runner to contact Carlos.

Rick told the Chief of the black hulled boat with the Mercury outboard.

The Chief said, "Pedro, bad man."

Mark arrived and was brought up to date.

They gave a twenty dollar bill and a lighter to the Chief.

He said thanks, and then said, "Do you have phone?"

Rick said, "Yes. I tried to call Carlos, but there was no answer."

The Chief said, "Runner get back he have number." He told them where to put their tents. He said, "No canoe more today. Wait for Carlos to say."

Later the runner returned. He said, "I have number."

Rick called the number and told Carlos what had happened. He also gave him a description of the black boat and the motor.

Carlos said, "I'll put out the description of Joan and the boat and outboard to my contacts. The police system is not local, but I'll alert them. I can send a car to pick Mark up so that he can work with me from this end. Rick, if we don't have a lead by morning, you may wish to canoe on to the next friendly landing, towing Mark's boat."

Mark had been listening since Rick had the phone on speaker phone. He said, "That sounds like a good plan."

"Be ready in an hour. They will bring you to me."

Rick said, "Let's be sure to keep in touch. Thanks for your help Carlos. We will do as you suggest."

Mark said, "I'll take my shotgun and a small amount of clothing."

The car came for Mark. They said goodbye, and he was gone.

Rick and Mary raised their tent and made a fire.

These natives had a large hut similar to the first one that they had seen.

Rick and Mary gave costume jewelry to each family.

The natives were friendly and smiled. These natives also used hammocks and had their own fires.

When they returned to their tent and sat down, the native women brought food to them. They thanked the women.

They were very concerned about Joan. They agreed to accompany each other whenever they left the camp site for any reason.

CHAPTER XII

CAPTURE

In the morning they thanked the Chief and made preparations to leave. The things in Mark's canoe were placed to balance the weight. The red canoe's bow was tied to the tan canoe's stern. They shoved off for the next friendly landing.

It rained, and they had difficulty handling the red canoe where the water was swift and rocks needed to be avoided. Rick had to pull the red canoe up close so that it would not go on the wrong side of the rocks.

About noon they beached the canoes to have lunch.

Mary said, "I'm worried about Joan. What if she got lost and we left her there alone among the savages?"

Rick replied, "I don't think she was lost. I am quite certain that she was abducted. Carlos and Mark are working together, and Carlos has contacts. Let's try to think of a positive outcome."

After a brief lunch, they walked around, and stretched, knowing that they would be sitting in the canoe for three or more hours.

Continuing down the river, Mary did her best to be positive, remarking about the animals and birds they saw. She was fascinated by the beautiful colors of the birds.

It was within an hour before dusk and they began to look for a place to stay the night. The next friendly camp was at least a full day away. They found a level spot without too much brush, and beached their canoes.

Rick asked Mary, "While I set up the tent and get a fire going, would you see if you could catch a fish or two?"

"Sure. I like the fishing chore."

Rick cleared a spot for the tent and then started a fire. He said, "I'm going to try to get Mark on the phone." The phone rang and Mark answered.

"Rick, is that you?"

"Yes, we just set up camp for the night. We are by ourselves. What is new on your end?"

"If our information is correct, the black hulled boat has not passed this location yet. I know that seems strange because that is a fast boat."

"Perhaps he had a contact somewhere before your location, and went through the forest. I am getting a lot of static Mark, I will have to hang up, but I plan to be at your location tomorrow evening." He said a quick goodbye and hung up.

He had been on speaker phone, so Mary had heard the conversation. She said, "If he had an accomplice and they went through the forest, how in the world would they ever catch him?"

"It might be impossible, but we will keep trying."

Just then Mary got a bite, and it was a real fighter. She let it wear itself out some, and then brought it in. It was a good sized fish and would be enough for a generous serving for each of them.

Rick complemented her on the handling of the catch.

After dinner they pulled the canoes close to the tent and set the alarms.

Rick said, "If we get an early start, we should be at the camp where Mark is before dusk."

In the morning, they packed up and launched the canoes. Once again they had a brief shower. At lunch time the wood was too wet to make a fire. They had a cold lunch, walked around and did some exercises.

They had paddled for about an hour and a half when Mary said, "I see something up ahead on the right. It may be a boat. Yes, it looks like that black hull boat."

They increased their speed and pulled up beside the boat.

Rick said, "That is the one, a black hull, and a Mercury outboard. Hurry! Let's tie up. Stay here Mary. Get out your pepper spray and guard the boats. I am going to track him down."

Rick took his shotgun and began tracking. He had years of experience in tracking. He found the trail and followed it, but then, knowing the general direction, he left the trail so that he could surprise Pedro.

A half hour later Mary heard Rick returning, but it wasn't Rick. It was the abductor and Joan. Joan's hands were tied behind her. Pedro saw that Mary was alone and quickly approached her.

Mary called out, "Joan duck down!" She used the pepper spray and it hit him in the eyes. He yelled, and let go of Joan to wipe his eyes.

Mary immediately went forward and kicked him as hard as she could in the groin. He fell to the ground. She got duct tape and taped his hands behind him. She wrapped it twice around his wrists, and then twice between his wrists and his hands. There was no way that he could get the tape off.

Mary took the binders off of Joan's wrists. They hugged as Joan wept. Mary asked, "What happened?"

Just then Rick returned. Mary told him what had happened.

Rick said, "That was wonderful Mary, I am so proud of you. Are you ok Joan? Can you tell us what happened?

"I'm not ok." Between sobs she related the story. "He grabbed me from behind and put a rag in my mouth. Then he tied my hands behind me, and took me back to his boat. At first he paddled to avoid making noise, but when we got further away he used the motor. We were going fast, but after a while the motor began to miss. He got it running, but later it finally quit. He couldn't get it started. He took me into the jungle and made camp for the night. He assaulted me."

Mary hugged her and said, "I am so sorry Joan."

Mary said. "Have you had anything to eat or drink?"

"No."

Mary said, "We can take care of that." She got food and drink for her.

Rick examined the duct tape. "You did a good job of tying him up. I will do the same with his ankles when I put him in the boat. We still need to go a considerable distance to get to the next landing where Mark is. Let's get ready to go, but first I will try to get Mark on the phone for you Joan."

The phone rang and Mark answered. "Mark, I have Joan here to talk to you. We are coming to you."

"Joan, I am so happy, I can't wait to see you. What happened?"

Joan said, "I'll tell you about it when I see you. I love you."

The volume became so weak, they said goodbye and hung up.

Rick said, I'll take the prisoner with me. Joan, would you please get in the bow of your boat, and Mary would you get in the stern of the red boat?"

Before getting in the canoe, Rick took the outboard motor off the black boat and dropped it in the river.

He took his shotgun and fired, creating holes in the bottom of the boat. It immediately began to take on water. He untied the boat and set it adrift. Rick said, "I will leave the prisoner to Mark to handle, but he will have a problem using that boat to kidnap someone again."

Rick put the prisoner in the bow facing aft, and taped his ankles. They paddled to get as much speed as possible. Just before dusk they arrived at the landing. Mark, Carlos and the natives were there laughing and cheering. It was a boisterous welcome.

Mark helped Rick get Pedro out of the canoe.

The canoes were beached.

The Chief came to welcome them. Rick gave him the usual gifts. He thanked them and showed them where they could put their tents.

Rick re-taped Pedro's ankles, laying him on the ground. The Chief said, "Leave him there. The medicine man will take care of him."

Rick and Mary set up the tents and brought the canoes up close. Mary set the alarms.

Mark and Joan went into the tent. Joan was crying as she told him all of the details including the rape.

Mark said, "I am so sorry honey. I will do what I can to make him pay for his cowardly act."

Joan said, "I can't stop trembling. What if he has a disease?"

Mark hugged her and said, "I will ask Carlos to take us in the car so that you can see a doctor."

Mark explained to Carlos what had happened to Joan, and asked Carlos about transportation to a doctor.

Carlos said, "Yes, we can do that in the morning. Be ready about 7:30. We had better take Pedro along. They will want to examine him and take blood samples."

Mark thanked him and went to talk with Rick.

Rick described to Mark what he had done to the boat to prevent it from being used in that fashion again. He said that he had not harmed the prisoner, leaving that decision to Mark.

Mark asked Rick's opinion as to what the law would do.

Rick said, "Maybe the law will get after him for kidnaping, but I doubt if they will do anything about the rape. It would be too hard to prove, just her word against his. He is a native, and she is a foreigner. I could be wrong. I suggest that you speak with Carlos. He knows how things work here."

"I'll ask him right now."

"Carlos what do you think the law would do about the kidnapping and the assault?"

Carlos said, "They may charge him with kidnapping. If so, the trial may be a year or more away, and all of you would need to be there to testify. There is nothing to prove rape, and I believe that they will not charge him for it."

Mark said to himself, "Then I will have to take care of it."

They met Carlos at 7:30 in the morning. Mark put Pedro in the back and Joan in the front. He sat in the back with Pedro.

The doctor saw Pedro first. He took blood samples and then examined him. He determined that he had a disease, and treated him.

He next saw Joan and took her blood samples and examined her. He said, "Tell me what happened." Joan related the events, and said that her nerves were shattered. The doctor said, "Pedro has a venereal disease and it may be transmitted to you. I will give to you an injection, and something to settle your nerves. I will need to see you in one week for a follow up."

Joan thanked the doctor and they left.

Mark attached the restraints to Pedro and they drove back to the camp.

Joan told Rick and Mary what she and Mark had learned from the doctor.

Mary said, "I don't think that we will need to stay here for a week. Any doctor can do the follow up. I suggest that we ask Carlos about the availability of a doctor further on our journey."

Mark said, "Yes. We need to get away from Pedro and the incident, and get some normalcy back into Joan's life." I'll speak to Carlos about that."

Mark took Rick aside and said, "Carlos says that they will not charge him with the rape. I don't want him to get away with it Scott Free, so I am going to take care of it."

Rick said, "If you need any help, I am ready."

Mark said, "I am going to take him away from camp into the forest. Don't let anyone follow me."

"OK."

Mark took the restraints from the prisoner's ankles and led him into the forest where he found a small clearing. It was some distance from the camp. He removed the restraints and told him to massage his wrists. Then he told him that he knew he had raped his wife and had possibly passed on his venereal disease to her. He said, "I am twice your age, but I am going to beat the tar out of you."

The prisoner massaged his wrists, but then began to run. Mark overtook him and drug him back to the clearing. Mark followed through with his threat. He took his time and proceeded to wreak his vengeance. Pedro kicked, threw punches, and tried to circle around Mark, but Mark was passionate in doing his duty. He began at the head. He heard the snap as Pedro's nose broke and saw the blood spurting. Then he began on his chest, arms and stomach.

The prisoner dropped to the ground. Mark picked him up and said, "You're not getting away that easily." He continued the beating, and saw Pedro spitting out teeth.

When Mark had completed the punishment, he told him. You will be charged with kidnapping. I hope that you go to jail for many years. This beating is for raping my wife. I believe that you will remember this beating for many years also."

Mark replaced the restraints on his wrists, and led him back to camp where he replaced the restraints on his ankles.

Rick looked him over, and said, "Mark, I believe that you did a bang up job."

Mark laid Pedro on the ground, leaving him for the medicine man and then said, "I will talk with Carlos."

"Is there a doctor further along our journey that we could see to get a follow up for Joan?

"Yes, let me consult the map I gave to you. Here it is, a friendly tribe has a doctor nearby. If you canoe six hours each day, it will take you about six days. You will recognize the area because the camp is on the outside of the curve in the river. Opposite the camp, on the other side of the river, is a huge black rock, about five feet high."

"Thanks, we'll plan to do that."

Carlos said, "I have notified the law, and they should arrive tomorrow. I believe they will want Joan to fill out a complaint form before you leave."

"I don't know what we would do without you during this emergency."

"That's my job. Have a good evening."

Mark told the others what he had learned. It was late afternoon, and they decided to rest before dinner.

Later, four women brought food on leaves for them. They thanked the women, and then Mary said, "This is similar to what the other tribe gave to us. It is good."

After dinner, Mary and Joan walked among the natives, handing out jewelry and saying hello. The natives also smiled and some said thanks.

In the morning they made preparations to leave, and then waited to be questioned and to fill out legal statements.

The law arrived and spoke to Pedro first. Pedro refused to provide any information about the kidnapping. He did tell that Mark had beaten him.

Joan was interviewed next, and was asked to sign a statement.

Then Mary, Rick and Mark were interviewed. The officer asked Rick about the prisoner's boat. Rick said, "We left it on the river where we found the prisoner and Joan." He and Mary were then asked to sign a statement.

The officer then asked Mark about the black eyes and broken nose of the prisoner. Mark said, "I did that to him. He kidnapped and raped my wife. It turns out that he has a venereal disease that he may have passed on to her. I had been told that he would not be charged with the rape since there was no way to prove it. I didn't want him to get away with this cowardly act without punishment, so I punished him.

The officer said, "The birds are so noisy here that I wasn't able to hear all of what you said, but I gather that he had an accident. I also had difficulty in hearing all that the prisoner had to say. I have all the information that I need. If there is a trial regarding the kidnapping, all of you will be asked to testify. Without your testimony the outcome of the trial would be questionable. That is all that I need now. Good luck on your canoeing.

The officer took Pedro and left.

They said goodbye to the Chief and thanked him for his hospitality. They waved to the natives and shoved off. Many of the natives came to watch them leave, and waved to them.

Chapter XIII

NEW FRIENDS

Joan said to Mark, "I don't think that I can stay for the full thirty days." She cried and said, "I am so upset. I can't get the assault out of my mind."

Mark said, "I understand. If you wish, we can leave after the doctor sees you."

Before lunch time, Mary said, "Look, there are some large puddles to the right of the tributary. Perhaps there are fish trapped there."

Rick said, "Let's tie up and see. He motioned for Mark and Joan to pull over.

They tied the canoes to the brush and got out. Joan said, "I see one, and there is another one near it."

Rick said, "Let's start at the end of the water on the side away from the fish and walk towards them. We will have to herd them to the shallow part, and scoop them out with our hands."

They all took their shoes off and waded side by side. They scooped three fish up and tossed them onto land.

Fish were picked up and placed in the canoe. Shoes were put back on and they resumed canoeing until they found an area that was fairly clear of shrubs. They tied up and Rick made a fire. Mary cleaned and cooked the fish.

Joan got paper plates. They had a tasty lunch, and after walking and stretching they resumed paddling.

At times the river had widened and was free of rocks. Then they were able to paddle side by side, and talk without shouting. The time went by quickly and they began to look for a place to land and camp for the evening. Once again they were going single file and Mary said, "I see something ahead, and I believe that it is a boat. Yes, it looks like a dugout canoe."

Rick said, "Let's take a chance and stop to see if it is a friendly native."

They tied their canoes beside the wood canoe. They saw a native man and woman, both wearing shorts. They had a fire going and were roasting something on a spit.

Rick called "Hello" to them and the natives returned the greeting. The man waved for them to come closer. The woman smiled. As they drew close, it looked like a pig was being roasted.

The native man met them and offered to shake hands. He said, "My name is Fernando, and my wife's name is Julia." The canoers offered their names, and told the natives about their journey, and why they had stopped.

Fernando said, "We are camping here for a few days. I shot the pig. You can join us. There is more food than we can eat."

Rick said, "Would you mind if we camped here with you tonight?"

"That would be fine."

Julia said, "Yes, I would like to talk with the ladies." She then excused herself, went into their tent and put on a shirt.

Rick and Mark brought the canoes up on the land, and then went back to talk with Fernando and his wife.

Rick asked, "Are you members of a tribe in this area?"

Fernando said, "No, we're actually on vacation. We live in Manaus. Once each year we live near the river and hunt and fish as we once did full time."

Mark said, "We flew from Alaska to Manaus. There we met our Brazilian contact. He took us to a tributary where we started our one month of canoeing."

Julia said, "When we are on vacation we dress and hunt and fish as the other natives do. In the city we have jobs and dress as others do there."

Rick asked, "How did you kill the pig?"

"I used my bow and arrow. I kept a number of things from the days when I was a member of a tribe. The bow and arrows, and my spear were the most important items."

Julia asked Mary and Joan, "Do you have jobs in Alaska?"

Mary said, "No, this is a big exciting adventure for us."

Joan said, "You speak English so well, do you speak other languages as well?"

Julia said, "Portuguese is our first language, but most natives speak some English. We took a course in conversational English before we got jobs."

Fernando said, "It looks like the meat is ready. Do you have plates and utensils?"

Mary and Joan said yes, and quickly got paper plates and utensils from the canoes.

Fernando put meat on each of their plates.

Rick said, "This looks and smells so good. We have been eating fish, and this is a delightful change."

Mary said, "We have salt and pepper." She offered it to all.

Julia said, "We normally bring along some fruit and vegetables. Today we have bananas for desert."

Mark asked, "Did you bring the canoe all the way from your home?"

"No, we have friends from a tribe about one half day's paddling, near here. We borrow his canoe. You should probably not stop there, they are hostile to strangers."

Rick asked, "Fernando, I am almost 49 years old. Do you mind telling me your age?"

"I am 26. Natives in tribes normally do not live beyond the age of 35. Until I got to Manaus I had never known anyone as old as you are. I believe that diet, constant exposure to the elements, and the lack of modern medical help has a lot to do with it."

When they finished eating the meat, Julia gave each of them a banana. They all enjoyed the meal and thanked Fernando and Julia.

Rick and Mark erected the tents and brought the canoes up close.

They sat around Fernando's fire and talked.

Mary asked, "Was it difficult for you to leave the tribe for a job in the city?"

Julia said, "Yes, the other natives felt that we were rejecting them personally as well as rejecting the life style."

Fernando said, "They made it very difficult for us, and some who had been friends, are no longer our friends. We have adjusted to our new life, and the yearly vacation by the river is all that we need of our former life style. Are you men retired?"

Rick said, "No, I am a writer for a sports magazine, and Mark owns and operates gold mines."

Fernando was excited, and asked Mark many questions about the gold mines.

When the mosquitos arrived they sprayed each other and put green leaves on the fire.

Rick asked, "Do you know Manuel?"

"Yes, he and his wife are friends of ours. How do you know them?"

"We met them while canoeing. We had dinner with them and with the Chief. It was an enjoyable meeting."

After more talking they put the alarms on the canoes and went to bed.

In the morning they thanked their hosts for their hospitality. They gave Fernando a lighter, and several pieces of jewelry to Julia. They got an early start after having leftover ham for breakfast and saying goodbye.

It was on their mind that they needed to arrive at the landing of the friendly natives for Joan to get her update from the doctor. For this reason they made haste. They did not take time to hunt, but the fish were plentiful, and they had their reserve food.

The days passed quickly.

CHAPTER XIV

PARTING

Up ahead they saw the large black rock, and opposite it the landing. They beached their canoes as children excitedly announced their arrival. Adults appeared and helped them bring their canoes up on dry land.

The Chief arrived, welcomed them with a handshake and a big smile. He said, "Welcome, we have been looking forward to meeting you since Carlos told us that you were coming. Let me show you where you can put your tents." He wore shorts and a short sleeve shirt. He did not have paintings on his face, and his smile was infectious.

They gave the chief the usual gifts. He thanked them and asked how he could help them.

Mark said, "My wife needs to see a doctor. Would it be possible to arrange transportation to and from his office?"

"Yes. I will arrange to have transportation for her the first thing tomorrow morning. I will be available if you have further questions." He waved and left.

Rick said, "That was a nice welcome. Let's move the boats near the place he showed us and erect the tents."

Two of the teenage boys came forward and helped them move the canoes. They remarked about the light weight, and asked to be told about the canoes. They felt the smooth siding with their hands. Rick told them about the materials used and the benefits of strength and maneuverability. Rick thanked them for their help, and the boys withdrew to the large hut.

Mark and Rick erected the tents while Mary and Joan found wood for a fire. That attended to, they went to the large hut and handed out costume jewelry to the natives.

It was dusk when they sat near the fire. Women from the large hut came bearing their dinner on large leaves. The meal contained vegetables, as the previous ones did, but in addition it contained meat. They thanked the women, and began to eat.

Mary said, "This is delicious, it tastes somewhat like turkey, but has a slightly different flavor.

Joan said, "You are right, it is delicious, and I can't tell what kind of bird it is from."

As one of the native walked by, Mary asked, "Can you tell me what kind of meat this is?"

She replied, "Like wild turkey. Name is Paruri."

Mary said, "Thanks, it is delicious."

In the morning Joan and Mark were taken to the doctor. Joan said that she was here for a follow up visit, and told what had happened. Blood was drawn and the doctor told her to call his number after lunch time tomorrow for the results.

When they returned to the native village, Joan told Rick and Mary that they would need to wait for the results of the blood sample until tomorrow after lunch, and that they would be going home then.

Rick said, "We will miss you, but while we wait, we are with friendly natives, and we all need a day of rest. Let's enjoy our leisure."

Mary said, "We are sorry that you are leaving, but we understand."

Joan said, "We hope to see you back in Alaska."

Mary said, "Perhaps we can. Let's talk with the native cooks."

Joan went along with her.

Rick said to Mark, "Let's go hunting and see what we can find in the forest."

Mark replied, "Sounds good to me. It is safe here for the women. I suggest that we get a guide to point out things that we might miss."

The Chief said, "Two of the teen age boys who helped you with your canoes would be perfect as your guides. They are very familiar with all types of animals, and they are interested in you and your journey. He called the boys. Francisco was sixteen years old. Geraldo was fifteen. "Both of these boys are experts with their bows and arrows, spears, and blow guns."

Rick and Mark shook hands with the boys and Rick said, "We would appreciate your guiding us through the forest telling us about the animals, and demonstrating the use of your weapons."

The boys were happy to demonstrate their skills, and gave them a tour of the area.

Upon their return to camp each boy was given five one dollar bills.

Francisco and Geraldo were excited. Francisco said, "Oh boy! This is the first money that I have ever had. Thanks." And away they ran to tell about their money.

After lunch the next day Joan received the good news that she did not have a disease.

They talked about leaving and what to take with them.

Mark said, "We'll take the canoe, paddles life jackets, pepper spray and the shotgun. We will leave our supplies with you. Our things will be shipped to our home so that we will not have to take it with us. We will be leaving the first thing in the morning."

That evening they reminisced about the good experiences of the trip

In the morning they all met to say their goodbyes.

Rick said, "We have all become very good friends, and we will miss you. I don't know when, but someday we will see you again."

Mark said, "Come visit us in Alaska, and plan to stay for a while."

Joan said, "I am so sorry that I must leave. I love you."

Mary said, "I hope that after a time, the pleasant memories of our canoe trip will be remembered far more than the negative one."

After hugs and saying goodbye, Mark and Joan left.

CHAPTER XV

JOURNEY RESUMED

Rick and Mary were sad at their leaving.

Rick said, "Almost three weeks have passed since we began our river adventure. How do you feel about it?"

"Putting the kidnapping aside, I have enjoyed being with you, Mark and Joan. I loved the canoeing, the fishing, making new friends and learning about the natives. It is a marvelous, once in a lifetime experience."

He smiled and said, "Then I take it that I won't be continuing our adventure by myself."

"That's right. There is no way that you get to keep all of the fun to yourself."

"Atta girl, I hoped that you would say that. Let's pack our canoe, and get to it."

They said goodbye to the Chief and shoved off. The natives waved goodbye.

As they paddled along, Rick said, "In time Joan will be able to resume her lifestyle and once again be happy, although she will never forget the assault. Now

89

we will need to put that past us and enjoy the rest of our adventure."

This turned out to be a beautiful day to canoe on the Amazon. It didn't rain. They laughed as they avoided rocks and whirlpools. Mary marveled at the beauty of the birds and the scenery. They saw an anteater and wild hogs.

At lunch time they beached the canoe at a small landing.

That evening they again found a suitable landing. Rick shot a bird about the size of a chicken, which they had with rice for dinner.

They had not seen another human from the time they left the native camp until they stopped for the night. It was a day for the pure enjoyment of the river and nature.

The next evening they stopped at a friendly camp. The natives and their Chief welcomed them. Their chief was dressed in shorts and a short sleeve shirt. He wore flowers around his neck, but did not have facial markings or animal teeth. He was friendly and showed them where to set up their tent.

Rick gave him the usual gifts. The Chief was pleased and told them that after their tent was set up he would give them a tour.

They pulled the canoe to the tent location, set up the tent, and set their alarm.

The Chief took them on tour. There was one main hut similar to those they had seen before. This is where the natives lived. Each family had their space near the perimeter with bamboo partitions between for some privacy. Most of the natives wore shorts or skirts, and shirts.

Mary handed out jewelry to each family.

Behind the living quarters was another hut that was used for meetings and for group dinners.

After completion of the tour the Chief said, "Come to the dining hut in about one half an hour. I would like for you to be my guests at dinner."

They said thanks, and went to their tent.

At dinner the Chief introduced his wife Luiza. He asked them to tell why they were canoeing, what they had enjoyed, and what they intended to do when they resumed their journey.

Rick said, "We enjoyed the white water canoeing, the fishing and seeing how the natives lived."

Mary told them about Joan's unfortunate incident. Mary said, "We will continue canoeing, and then go by land to Manaus before going to the States."

The Chief remarked that since they did not have local law, some of the uncivilized natives took advantage of the situation, leaving a bad impression that all natives were like that.

They assured him that they had been in camps where the natives were very friendly and helpful, including his. They said that they intended to see two native couples when they reached Manaus.

Rick asked if the Chief knew Carlos.

"Yes, I know Carlos. We are friends and sometimes we visit each other. If you get in a jam let one of us know, and we well do our best to be helpful."

Mary and the Luiza chatted while Rick talked further with the Chief. They thanked the Chief for the tour, and Luiza for the dinner. They said goodnight.

Mary said, "That was so pleasant. We have had several perfect days in a row, but I am tired and could use a good night's sleep."

Rick agreed and they turned in.

In the morning they struck the tent, and prepared to leave.

The Chief and many natives came to see them off.

They said goodbye.

MOTORBOAT THIEVES

That afternoon they heard a motor boat approaching from the rear. Rick unstrapped his shotgun, which he had kept loaded, and placed it beside him, but out of sight. Since he was not going to shoot birds, the shotgun was loaded with slugs, suitable for shooting larger game. He said, "Have your pepper spray ready, but out of sight before the boat catches up with us."

The motor boat pulled up alongside them, but about ten or twelve feet away, and slowed to their pace. There were two natives dressed in shorts. The man in the stern was large and had animal teeth around his nose and ears. The second man was smaller but had similar features and ornaments.

The large native said, "That's a nice boat. You must be rich. I'd like to have that boat."

Rick said, "Yes it is a nice boat but it is not for sale. Where are you headed?"

"We don't want to buy it. Maybe you give it to us."

"No, we need the boat, and you already have one."

"I think maybe you will give it to us, or maybe we just take it."

"No. Why don't you just motor on and leave us alone?

"No, what do you mean No? Pull over at this little clearing and talk!"

Rick brought out his shotgun and said, "We are not going to pull over, and we don't want to talk. Move on."

The big man laughed and said, "You got a gun but you gringos don't shoot."

Rick raised the shotgun and shot at short range at the middle of the boat between the two men. It put a hole in the hull and the water began to come into the boat.

"You crazy man! You put a hole in our boat! Now we get you!"

Rick shot another hole in their boat and said, "If I shoot again it will be at one of you. Which one wants to be shot first?"

The natives scurried to put something in the holes to stop the flow of water.

Rick said, "You know that I will shoot you if I have to. Move on and leave us alone."

The man in the rear of the boat started to move the boat away while the other man tried to plug the holes. He shook his fist at Rick and said, "We'll get you."

As they left, Mary said, "I'm so scared, and he said he would get us."

Rick said, "We will have to be alert. I believe that they will try to get even." He reloaded his shotgun.

That evening they saw a small area that had a good bit of vegetation, but this time it served their purpose. They beached the canoe, and immediately put it behind shrubs so that it would not be visible from the river. Mary began fishing while Rick put the tent up, also behind vegetation, and gathered wood for a fire.

Mary caught a nice fish and cooked it over the small fire.

While they ate, Mary said, "Do you think that we should go back to the friendly camp and report the incident to the Chief and Carlos?"

Rick said, "Going against the current would take us more than a day to get there, and we would still have to come this way again anyhow. I believe that we'll be ok if we are alert. We certainly have had an exciting adventure so far." He put out the fire.

Mary said, "Yes, it has never been dull, but I could do with a little bit more peace and relaxation, and fewer wild uncivilized natives."

They looked at their map and saw that they had less than a week more to go before they would arrive at their final landing.

They set the alarm on the boat and turned in for the night.

In the morning, Rick said, "No more hiding from now on. We'll deal with them face to face. We'll win out in the end."

Mary said, "I'm scared. I hope that you are right."

They shoved off and had a delightful morning, until they rounded a curve in the river and saw a rope. It was stretched tight across a narrow part of the river and it was secured to the land on each side. The rope was about one foot above the river surface, and it would prevent them from going further.

From their right side came a voice, "We've got you this time Gringo. You can't get beyond the rope, and we have a big surprise for you when you get out of your boat."

Rick noticed that their boat was tied up to the bank, on the right side, some 30 feet or more beyond the rope. Rick said, "Let's turn around and go up stream until I think this out."

Mary said, "What kind of a surprise do they have?"

Rick said, "Probably a trap of some kind."

They turned around, went upstream about 40 yards and turned down stream again.

Rick said, "Let's jump over the rope."

Mary said, "How can we do that?"

"When we get close to the rope, move back to the middle of the boat, and then lean back to put more weight to the rear. We must paddle fast towards the rope. Just before we get to it I will jump up, off of the boat, and then land hard on the stern with all of my weight. That should momentarily raise the bow enough so that we can canoe over the rope. The bow curves up from below the water line to the top of the bow. That will help. I noticed that the rope dips a bit towards the center, and we will aim for that point. Now let's paddle as fast as we can."

They raced towards the center of the rope. Rick said, "NOW!" Mary moved back, Rick jumped up and dropped his weight on the stern seat. The bow raised about six inches or so, for a few seconds, the curved bow slid up and over the rope. They were on top of the rope.

Rick said, "Paddle Mary, paddle fast!"

Arrows zipped around them.

Rick got this shotgun and aimed at the waterline of the native's boat as they crossed over the rope. He felt two arrows hitting him, one in the arm and the other in his back. He fell forward into the river. Mary screamed and looked for him. When he did not come up for air, she dove into the water and pulled him to the surface. She got behind him and put her left arm around his chest. With a side stroke, she swam with him to the bank away from the natives. Rick was not conscious

The natives ignored Rick and Mary. They jumped into their boat and tied the canoe to its stern. Without a backward glance they proceeded down the river with their prize.

After a while Mary was able to arouse Rick. She asked if he was ok. He said, "Sort of. I'm kind of dizzy. What happened?"

Mary said, "Two poisoned arrows hit you just as you were about to shoot their boat. You passed out and fell into the river. I jumped in and towed you to the shore. The natives took our boat and towed it down the river."

"Thanks Mary. Were you able to bring anything with you?

"No, but you had a death grip on the shotgun, and it is still in your hand. Do you have anything else with you"

My knife is still attached to my belt, and I feel the zippo lighter in my pocket. I will drain the water out, but the lighter fluid will be drained also."

"What will we do Rick?"

"I'll need a few minutes to let the poison wear off and get my brain working. Oh wait, I feel the cell phone. It will be soaked and worthless until I can get a new battery. I also still have my wallet. The money will be soaked, but the credit cards will be ok. Let's walk around for a couple of minutes to bet my blood circulating."

After about five minutes Rick said, "I feel better now. I believe that we should walk back to the friendly village and ask the Chief and Luiza for their help."

"That's going to take a while."

"Yes, it might take two days, and we don't have a tent, food, or a lighter to start a fire. I don't see another alternative."

"I don't either, so if you feel up to it we had better get started."

They started out, keeping close as possible to the river. The undergrowth was thick and it was slow going. Mary slapped a mosquito and said, "On the river we were not bothered by mosquitos, but they are here on land, and we don't have any spray."

Rick said, "I forgot to tell you that when the boys, Francisco and Geraldo, took Mark and I into the forest they told us of a plant that they used to discourage the mosquitos. As we walk along I'll look for it."

Later Rick found the plant and they used the sap on their skin. It was helpful, but not as effective as mosquito spray.

After walking for a few hours they stopped to rest. Rick found a straight branch about five feet long and about an inch and one half in diameter. At one end the limb branched out and formed a V. He cut these at about three inches. This pole was for defensive purposes, but also as a device to hold a snake, if they found one. As he worked on the pole he said, "If we don't find food during for the next two days, it will not be seriously harmful to our health. Water will be our big problem. This close to the river we are not likely to find fresh water, and we have no way to boil it. We'll have to hope for rain."

They continued walking, jumping over and around trees and brush.

Mary saw a snake and pointed it out to Rick. They had seen other snakes, but most were too small to eat. It was about four feet long and had a diameter of about two inches.

Rick cautiously came up behind it and quickly put the V of the pole behind the snakes head. He then thought, we can't cook the meat and I don't think that we want to eat raw meat. He lifted the pole and the snake scampered away. He said, "Have a good life little snake."

After another three hours of walking they stopped for the night. Rick made a lean to, cutting small trees to provide a frame. Mary stacked large leaves and small branches over the frame as Rick cut them.

They saw various types of birds, but they did not have a way to kill them or to cook them for dinner.

Mary said, "I feel very angry about the natives shooting you and taking our canoe. What do you think we can do about it?"

"I agree with you. I don't want to let them get away with it. Even if we had a canoe we could not catch up with them. Let's think more about it. We will need to talk with Carlos. We will need something faster than a canoe."

Mary said, "Could we afford a helicopter?"

"That's it, a helicopter. Good thinking. Yes, we can afford it. We'll see if one is available."

Leaves were gathered and strewn on the floor of the lean to. Mosquito sap from the plant was reapplied. They curled up and attempted to sleep.

The next day was a repetition of the first day except that it rained about noon time. They used leaves to catch the water and guide it into their mouth.

That evening they reached the friendly village and met with the Chief and Luiza. They took a shower in the Chief's hut and were served a fine dinner.

The Chief said, "Tell me what happened."

Rick and Mary told the story.

The Chief asked, "What do you intend to do, and how can I help you?"

Rick said, "My cell phone was soaked and is inoperable. I would like to call Carlos, if I may use your phone."

The Chief readily agreed and dialed the number for Rick.

"Hello Carlos, this is Rick. We are here with the Chief and Luiza. We had terrible time with some natives who took our canoe. We need some help."

"Of course Rick. I want to hear the whole story, but tell me what you can now, and how I can help you."

"Mary and I want to get those guys and our canoe and its contents." He provided Carlos with a description of the natives, their boat, and his canoe. If you could alert the police to keep an eye out for them it would be helpful. Second, we will need at least the following: Ammunition for my shotgun, slugs, not bird shot. Two binoculars, One can of pepper spray for Mary, a small can of lighter fluid, and a battery for my cell phone. He gave the number and description of the battery to Carlos. I would like to have a helicopter pick Mary and I up here, as soon as possible, bringing along the items that I listed. They already have a two days start on us."

Rick, there is a helicopter in Manaus, but it will be very expensive. Possibly more than your canoe and equipment is worth.

"The expense is no problem Carlos. We are angry and want to do what we can to make things right. They shot me with poisoned arrows."

"I'll check on the helicopter right away and call you back. I will personally find the items you want."

"Thanks Carlos, we very much appreciate your help. I'll wait for your call.

The Chief said, "What can we do in the meantime to help you?"

Rick said, "Providing a place for us to rest up, eat and make phone calls has been a life saver. There is really nothing more that I could ask for. My wallet needs some attention. The cash needs to be carefully separated and dried. My cell phone needs to have the battery removed, and the interior dried.""

Mary offered, "I'll take care of the cell phone."

The Chief went with Rick to take care of the wallet, and Luiza went with Mary to help with the cell phone.

Mary asked Luiza for a tablespoon of uncooked rice to put in the cell phone to draw the moisture out.

Within a half an hour Carlos called. He said, "The helicopter is available, and the pilot is pleased to get the business. He wants to call you to confirm details and to discuss his fees. He will call you within the next fifteen minutes. In the meantime, I'll get started on the items that you need."

"Thanks Carlos, I'll wait for his call."

The pilot called. His name was Arnos. He asked Rick what he wanted to do, and how long it would take.

Rick told him that he wanted to locate two men who had stolen his canoe. He did not know how long it would take.

The pilot discussed his rates by the hour and by the day, and asked how Rick intended to pay for it.

Rick told him that he would use a credit card, and said that he wanted the daily rate. He asked how soon the pilot could start.

"I can start the first thing tomorrow morning. It is too late now to start. Carlos told me where you are and gave me a map. like the one he gave to you of the river and some landings. I should be at your location between 7:30 and 8 o'clock.

They said goodbye.

Rick told them all of the conversation.

Rick and Mary continued on their chores of the cell phone and the wallet.

After breakfast they all waited for the arrival of the pilot. When they heard the helicopter coming Rick and Mary thanked their hosts and said goodbye.

CHAPTER XVII

HELICOPTER

It was a few minutes before 8 AM.

Introductions were made and the pilot produced the items that Rick had ordered.

Rick examined the items. He loaded the shotgun and Mary installed the new battery in the cell phone.

Rick explained to the pilot what had happened and described the natives, their boat and his canoe. He asked to see the map that Carlos had given to him. Pointing at the map he said, "This is where they took our canoe. I believe that that they should be at about this point, and he pointed to a new location further down the river.

The pilot said, "With their motor boat, don't you think that they could be much further than that?

Rick said, "Their speed will be determined by the hull speed of the canoe. If they go too fast the canoe will overturn. They also have to be careful that the canoe does not go on the wrong side of a large rock, or get caught in a whirlpool."

Mary took one set of binoculars and Rick took the other. Mary sat behind the pilot and watched on that side. Rick sat beside the pilot and watched on his side.

As they passed the location where their canoe was taken they saw the rope still stretched across the river.

They proceeded slowly around the spot where Rick thought they might be, but saw nothing. He asked the pilot to continue on for about five miles. No luck.

Rick said, "Let's retrace our route and go slow above any landing, no matter how small. It is possible that they hid the canoe temporarily." Once again they saw nothing to help them.

Rick said, "Let's continue on down the river. I must be wrong in my assumptions as to their location."

The next landing was one that Carlos had said was one of friendly natives.

Rick said, "Land here, I want to talk with the Chief."

After landing it seemed like the entire village came to see what was going on. Rick asked to speak with the Chief.

The Chief appeared and welcomed them. He asked, "How can I help you?"

Rick explained what had happened, and describe the men and the boats. He asked if the Chief had seen the men or their boat.

The Chief said, "The men you described stopped here briefly late last evening with their motor boat. They did not have a canoe with them."

Rick said, "Then it is possible that they hid the boat somewhere while proceeding without it."

The chief said, "How can I help you?"

Rick said, "Do you have two men who are familiar with the area, that you trust, who could search the area for several miles on each side of the river, looking for a hidden canoe? I will be glad to pay them for their time."

The Chief said, "Let me talk alone with some of my men to see who might be interested in the search."

He called a half a dozen men to come with him. They withdrew out of hearing range.

The Chief said, "A canoe was taken from these people. We believe that the men who came by here last evening took their canoe and temporarily hid it somewhere up river. Would any of you men be interested in searching for them? They will pay you for your work."

Four men raised their hands.

The Chief said, "Hosea and Edwardo know that area best. You two come with me."

He introduced the men to Rick.

Rick said, "Thanks for helping. I will pay you whether you find the canoe or not, and I will give an additional bonus to the one who finds it. I want one of you to cover the other side of the river. I want you two to keep in sight and calling distance of the other. We will keep sight of you from the air. Do you have any questions?

Edwardo said, "What does the canoe look like?"

It is tan in color, about 20 feet long, and when it was taken it had a good deal of equipment and supplies in it."

Hosea immediately went to the other side of the river. Both men then began to go upstream.

They thanked the Chief for his assistance and boarded the helicopter.

Rick said, "Let's go back again to the location that I thought they might be at, and do a more slow and thorough visual inspection."

Rick asked the pilot, "Do you have a megaphone, or some way of talking to those on the land as we fly over?"

"Yes, it is a very good one that can clearly be heard for several hundred yards."

They arrived at the location and slowly circled. Unfortunately, the vegetation was very thick beyond the large landing. It was not possible to make a determination.

Let's go down stream again to make eye contact with the two men, and then proceed downstream past the village that we just visited."

They found the two men opposite each other. Rick used the Plane's phone to call to the men. He said, "Any luck." The men said no.

They went down river past the village about five miles when they saw a motor boat going upstream fairly fast.

Rick said, "Keep going, I don't want them to think that we are interested in them." He focused his binoculars on the boat. He said, "That's the boat."

Mary said, "And those are the two men."

Rick said, "Arnos, make a wide sweep so that those in the boat do not see you. I want to keep in occasional sight of the boat from a good distance. It is imperative that they do not suspect that the helicopter has anything to do with them. I will leave how we do that up to you."

Arnos said, "Don't worry I'll take care of that." He made a wide swoop and went inland quite a distance so that those in the boat could neither see nor hear the helicopter. Then he proceeded up stream.

Rick said, "I will want to be near them at the time they land so that we can see if they then get the canoe. Once the boat is beyond the village I want to tell the searchers to return to the village since we have sighted the boat."

Arnos took some time to be sure that the boat was well beyond the village. He then slowly went upstream behind the searchers until he saw them. He went low and hovered.

Rick called to the men. We have seen the boat. Please return to your village. I will come back to pay you later. Thank you for your help."

They all waved.

Rick said, "Now we want to keep the boat in sight from a distance so that we can see where it turns in. Then we will see if they retrieve our canoe"

Arnos kept the helicopter from sight and sound of the thieves.

The boat turned in at the landing that Rick had thought they might have hidden the canoe.

The natives secured their boat and went into the forest. Within minutes they were pulling the canoe towards the water.

Rick said, "Now Arnos, go directly over their boat and hover." He opened the door and shot holes in the bottom of the boat. He reloaded and shot additional holes. He took the loud speaker and called to the thieves, "Do not approach your boat. Move towards the river and put up your hands."

The thieves immediately ran into the forest out of sight.

Rick called Carlos on his Cell phone. "Carlos, this is Rick. We have found the thieves and their boat, and followed them to where they had hidden our canoe. Can you get police to pick them up?

Carlos said, "I will contact the police, but I cannot guarantee that they will be available. Where exactly are you?

Rick said, "The pilot can give you the exact location that the police will understand."

Arnos gave Carlos the location.

Rick said, "The thieves are out of sight. Land near the canoe and let us out. We need to see if the paddles and other equipment are still in the canoe."

As Arnos landed Rick reloaded his shotgun. They got out and immediately found that the paddles and other supplies were still in the canoe. Rick pulled the canoe to the water's edge while Mary pushed.

Rick saw that the thief's boat was filling with water. He then shot the motor and it blew into pieces.

He said to Arnos, "We will go by canoe to the village to pay the searchers. Meet us there.

They jumped into the canoe and swiftly began downstream.

Fifteen minutes later Carlos called. "Rick, as you know, there is no local police force in that area. Those that I contacted did not seem to be very interested."

"That's ok Carlos. We recaptured the canoe and are on the way to the village where we called you from. I disabled their boat and the men ran away into the forest. I will not prefer charges. I would appreciate it if you would update the police. Thanks for your help. We will keep in touch."

They arrived at the friendly village and paid the searchers twenty dollars each. The men were very thankful. They had no regular way of earning money. Rick also gave the chief the usual gifts.

Arnos was paid and told them that this was the most exciting job that he had in a long time. He flew to Manaus.

It was now nearly dark, and the Chief invited them to have dinner with them. The pilot had already told them what had happened, but the Chief asked them to tell their version of the incident. Later, the Chief also asked them to stay in his hut overnight since it was now dark.

In the morning after breakfast they said thanks to all and got underway downstream.

CHAPTER XVIII

FINAL LANDING

Let's take a couple of deep breaths to relax, and enjoy the rest of our adventure."

They did enjoy the rest of the day and the landing that they found in the evening.

The next few days were idyllic with canoeing, fishing and hunting. They didn't see another person until they arrived at their final landing.

They paddled into the beach at the clearing. Native children laughed and called a welcome to them. The native adults appeared with smiles and welcoming calls. They went ashore and asked to speak with the Chief.

The Chief smiled and welcomed them. He was tall and was neatly dressed with shorts and a short sleeve shirt. He did not have animal teeth around his face, or paintings on his face. He shook their hands and led them to an area where they could put their canoes.

Rick gave him their gifts.

The Chief thanked them.

Native boys pulled the canoe to the spot the Chief designated.

The Chief said, "I have been expecting you. Carlos told me about you and the problem that your friends had. I am sorry that happened. We will do our best for you. When you have set up your tent I will take you on a tour. Just come to the large hut. I will be there."

Rick set up the tent while Mary got jewelry out to give to the natives.

Rick called Carlos and said, "Carlos, we are at our last landing."

"Hello Rick, I'm glad that you made it safely. When do you want me to come to pick you up?"

"Tomorrow morning would be fine, if that suits you. What time do you want us to be ready?"

"About eight thirty. Would that be ok?"

"That's fine. We'll see you then."

They found the Chief in the large hut. It was very similar to one that they had seen before.

Mary gave jewelry to each family. The natives were appreciative.

The Chief then took them to another hut that was their meeting space and a place for group dining. The next hut was the Chief's residence. They met his wife Helena who said, "I would like to ask you to join us here for dinner. I have started to cook, and it should be ready in about half an hour. Please sit down. We can talk while I prepare dinner."

Mary said, "May I help you with the dinner in anyway?"

"No, but thanks, I would just like to hear some about your trip."

Rick said, "I believe that you have already heard about the kidnapping. Since then we have had another incident where two uncivilized natives took our canoe." He then proceeded to tell them the story.

The Chief said, "That was a dangerous situation, but you handled it well."

Mary said, "I am still frightened when I think of it."

Rick said, "It is over now and we are safe. I called Carlos and he will pick us up tomorrow morning to take us to Manaus."

They continued to talk while they had dinner. Later they returned to their tent for the night.

Carlos arrived, and all shared greetings. He said, "I hope your journey was pleasant and uneventful after retrieving your canoe."

They then told Carlos all of the details.

"I'm sorry that you had a second problem with these uncivilized natives, but you put them out of commission, and we will all be safer. Let's get things in my truck. It will take us until about one o'clock to get to the hotel in Manaus."

CHAPTER XIX

MANAUS, BRAZIL

Arriving at the hotel, Rick and Mary checked in to the same room that they had before. The hotel manager had held their clothing and other belongings for them.

Carlos would be sending the canoe and other items to their home in Norte Dakota. Rick settled his account with Carlos. They shook hands and said goodbye.

Mary said, "The first thing I want is a long shower."

"Me too, I'll join you."

Next on the agenda was a meal in the hotel.

Mary said, I don't want to eat fish. I believe I will have lasagna."

"Me either, but I believe a steak would hit the spot."

After dinner Rick called Manuel.

"Manuel, this is Rick. We have returned to Manaus from our adventure. How are things with you?"

"I'm glad to hear from you Rick. All is well here. Are you staying at a hotel?"

"Yes, we will be at the "Raquel Wellington, in the same room that we had before."

"That's great. Fernando called me and said that they had met you. We are free tomorrow after work, and I will call Fernando. He and his wife can join us, if that would suit you."

"That would be fine. We can profitably use the time between now and then to catch up on resting and making flight arrangements."

"Ok, I'll pick you up at your hotel tomorrow at 6:30."

Manuel and Ana Maria picked them up and said, "Fernando and Julia will be joining us at our place at about 7."

Mary said, "I'm so glad you were available on the spur of the moment. We were never certain as to when we would be here."

Fernando pulled up in his car just as they were exiting Manuel's car. Greetings and hugs were exchanged.

Rick said to Fernando and Julia, "It's so nice to see you again. This is a great way to end our Amazon adventure."

Ana Maria smiled and said, "Welcome to our home. Come in and make yourselves at home. We will be eating shortly, I ordered pizza."

"That's great," said Mary. "We haven't had pizza since we left Alaska.""

Fernando asked, "Would you tell us what you liked most on your adventure, and what you liked least?"

Mary answered, "There was so much that I liked: the canoeing, the scenery, the friendly natives, the fishing, seeing first hand a different culture, and the help that Carlos gave us, and meeting all of you. I'll ask Rick to tell you about the major problems that we had."

"The first problem when Joan was kidnapped and assaulted you already know. The second problem came from two men in a fast boat with a large motor who took our canoe from us." He then related the details of the two events.

Ana Maria said, "I am so sorry that you had these problems. There are a few tribes with very bad men, and there is no local law outside of the big cities. They get away with a lot."

Fernando said, "It looks like you were well able to take care of the problem. I think that we need you to be our sheriff."

Rick laughed and said, "We came through it all ok. The Amazon adventure was so worthwhile."

The pizza arrived, and beer was served.

Rick said, "The pizza is delicious, and the beer is tasty. What brand of beer is it?

"This one is Brahma. There are other beers that we like also. One is called Skol and the other one is Antarctica.

During dinner they talked, and again questions were asked about gold mining.

Rick answered them and then said, "You know, it is not only in your country where there are problems with bad men. We had problems with them in Alaska."

The talking continued until late in the evening.

Mary said, "I'm sure that you all need to go to work in the morning. It has been a wonderful visit with you, but it is time for us to go to the hotel." They said goodbye to Fernando, Ana Maria and Julia.

Manuel drove them to the hotel and asked them to keep in touch.

They thanked him and said that they would. They all said goodbye.

In their room they relaxed in comfort. Sitting on the couch, Mary cuddled up to him and he kissed her. They talked about their adventure.

Rick said, "We found the experiences and excitement that we had hoped for. I was especially pleased to experience firsthand a different culture. What about you Mary?"

"I very much enjoyed our farewell dinner with Manuel, Anna Maria, Fernando and Julia. That dinner with our native friends provided the perfect ending to our adventure."

I also loved the birds and the beauty of the rain forest. One of the things that make me feel so good is that although there was danger in the swift river with rocks and whirlpools, I learned how to manage it without fear, in fact, I enjoyed it."

"I know you did, and I was so pleased that you adapted so well to outdoor life. I know that next time we will be even more alert to potential problems. I was very pleased with our guide Carlos and our pilot Arnos."

Mary said, "I am looking forward to seeing Mark and Joan again.

Rick said, "Yes, and we will also have to prepare for our next adventure."

In the morning they flew back to the States.

THE END

Printed in the United States
By Bookmasters